FOREVER ISLAND

Novels by Patrick Smith

THE BEGINNING
ALLAPATTAH
ANGEL CITY
FOREVER ISLAND
A LAND REMEMBERED
THE RIVER IS HOME

FOREVER ISLAND

Patrick Smith

Pineapple Press, Inc.
Sarasota, Florida

Inquiries should be addressed to:

Pineapple Press, Inc.
P.O. Box 3889
Sarasota, Florida 34230

www.pineapplepress.com

Library of Congress Cataloging-in-Publication Data

Smith, Patrick D., 1927-
  Forever Island / Patrick Smith.
    p. cm.
  ISBN 978-1-56164-564-0 (hardback : alk. paper)
  1. Seminole Indians--Fiction. 2. Whites--Relations with Indians--
Fiction. 3. Everglades (Fla.)--Fiction. I. Title.
  PS3569.M53785F6 2012
  813'.54--dc23
                                    2012027515

First edition

Composition by Lubin Typesetting and Literary Services
Printed in the United States of America

FOREVER ISLAND

ONE

CHARLIE JUMPER stopped the dugout canoe in a pool of black water and watched the fish as it came out of a clump of pickerel weed. He picked up the spear and waited as the gar swam closer, its long snout poking into the decayed matter beneath it. It moved in a slow circle, coming nearer and nearer, until finally the old man smashed the spear into the side of the fish. He flicked the gar into the bottom of the dugout, put down the spear, and poled the canoe to the next clump of weeds.

He muttered, "Must have two gar. Little George might be hungry today." High overhead, a flight of crows cawed noisily as they winged their way eastward across the swamp. The old man stood rigidly erect, squinting into the still water, then again the spear slammed downward and a gar was brought into the dugout, its blood spilling over the bottom of the cypress canoe.

Once again the old man poled the dugout swiftly across the water, causing little waves to form behind and make rippling sounds as they spread outward into the cypress knees. He was moving deeper into the swamp, and the growths of live oaks, dwarf cypress, and cabbage palms, heavily laced with vines, blocked out the sun and caused the stream and the woods to be bathed with a soft yellowish tint. Ahead of him, the white heron lifted itself from the water's edge and glided away from his path, and the gallinule and rail scurried away into the grass.

The narrow stream turned and widened out with no visible bank, and at this point the old man turned right, entering an area of dwarf cypress and slimy water. The water mark on the cypress indicated that here there was normally two feet of water, but now the water was down to eight inches. The trunks of the trees were dotted with air plants, and scattered throughout the area were clumps of button bush and pickerel weed.

The old man traveled for a half mile across the green water and then turned into a slough covered with water lilies. This led into a pond of about two acres, most of the pond leading again into the dense swamp but the south portion covered by a mudbank. The dugout glided to within thirty feet of the mudbank and then stopped.

Lying atop the bank was a giant alligator at least eighteen feet in length, its body partially sunk into the muck. Aside from its size, it was different from any other alligator because of a scar that ran across the back of its head. Where its right eye had once been there was now a grotesque clump of scar tissue.

The old man and the alligator faced each other, the two eyes locking into the one eye as if in a greeting, then the man said, "You will eat now, Little George. I have brought you two nice garfish."

When the man threw one of the fish from the dugout, the alligator slid from the mudbank and came forward, his tail pushing him through the water. The fish made one brief chomp for his massive jaws, then the second garfish was thrown to him. When he finished this one he hesitated for a moment, waiting to see if more fish would come from the dugout, and then he turned and climbed back onto the mudbank, his one eye again locking into the eyes of the old man.

"You like it, heh, Little George," the man chuckled. "Next time I will also bring you a swamp rabbit. I will see you again in a few days."

The alligator continued to watch as the old man turned the dugout and started retracing his way across the pond and into the swamp.

Charlie Jumper was a Mikasuki Seminole, eighty-six years of age, living in the Big Cypress Swamp, the northern entrance to the Florida Everglades. His wiry body stretched only to five-nine, and his skin, baked deep brown by the many years of the Florida sun, resembled the bark of the cypress tree. His once black hair was now flecked with white.

Charlie Jumper had lived for the past sixty years at the same spot on the bank of Gopher Creek. He could remember once living in a glade deeper in the swamp, and he remembered an earlier life on a hammock in the River of Grass, but before that he was not certain.

He could not say for sure where he was born, but he knew he was a youth in early manhood when the century turned, and he could be older than the eighty-six years he claimed.

The old Indian now lived alone with his wife Lillie Tiger, but one mile away was the home of his youngest son, Billy Joe, and Billy Joe's family. Twenty-two years ago Billy Joe had gone to the real estate agent in Immokalee and asked if he could buy some of the land and put it to use. He had been told that the land was not for sale but that he could rent what he wished, and he had signed a rental agreement for ten acres at a cost of ten dollars per acre per year. Two acres of the land he had cleared for a truck farm, and on the rest he raised hogs and a few cows.

When Billy Joe had built the wooden frame house a mile away, his father had refused to come and live in the house. Billy Joe asked Charlie several times, but he finally accepted the fact that his father would never abandon the camp on the bank of Gopher Creek.

Billy Joe had married Watsie Cypress during a celebration of the Green Corn Dance, and now they had two children, Lucy, nineteen, and Timmy, twelve. Billy Joe was forty-two and Watsie five years younger.

Three other sons had been born to Charlie and Lillie Jumper. One was buried on a hammock in the marsh, and the other two had once gone to Oklahoma to attend an Indian trade school and had never returned.

In refusing to abandon the old ways, Charlie Jumper was not unique. There were many other Seminole chickees, or huts, on scattered hammocks throughout the Everglades and in remote sections of Big Cypress. The needs of these people were simple, and their lives were tied to the animals and the water and the land. They had no desire to live elsewhere. Charlie Jumper himself had no thought of leaving his chickees on the bank of Gopher Creek, for to him the swamp was eternal and indestructible.

When Charlie reached his camp he pulled the dugout onto the bank and began cleaning a black bass he had speared on the way home. Lillie was at her sewing machine on a small raised platform in the cooking chickee.

The Jumper camp was composed of a cluster of three chickees, one for sleeping, one for cooking and eating, and one for storage. Frames for the chickees were dwarf cypress poles, and the pointed roofs were made of palmetto fronds. The sleeping chickee had a raised cypress plank platform three feet off the ground, as did the storage one. The floor of the cooking chickee was dirt except for the small raised platform at the north end that served as Lillie's sewing area. The storage chickee had three palmetto frond walls, and the other two chickees were open on all sides.

In the center of the cooking chickee there was a large iron grate held up by two walls of limestone rock, and on the grate sat two skillets and a cast iron dutch oven. Under the inside eaves of the structure Charlie had constructed shelves which held the various pots and pans, such staples as coffee, sugar, salt, flour, and cornmeal, and the few canned goods that were purchased at the store in Copeland.

The chickees were built beneath a huge live oak, and the clearing was ringed by magnolia, dwarf cypress, cabbage palm, and wax-myrtle. There was a clump of banana trees that Charlie had planted, and a small plot of ground was used for growing corn, tomatoes, beans, squash, sweet and Irish potatoes, and cucumbers. A flock of chickens roamed the clearing, and off to one side there was a hog pen which was no longer used.

All of Lillie's time when not cooking was spent at the foot-pedal sewing machine, which had been given to her fifty years ago by a white woman who had opened an Indian mission in Everglades City. Lillie made colorful Seminole jackets, skirts, and blouses which Billy Joe sold for her to the souvenir stands along the Tamiami Trail. Her pieces always brought a good price, for she was one of the few Seminole women left who could hand-weave into the cloth the exact designs on the backs of the now almost extinct tree snails. Lillie would spend at least six hours each day on the sewing platform, and her work produced almost all of the cash money available for purchases of staples and cloth.

Most of Charlie's time was spent roaming the swamp and marsh in search of fish, turtles, squirrels, rabbits, turkey, and ducks. It was seldom any more that he hunted the swift deer or the bear. He also gathered the guavas, blueberries, wild grapes, plums, blackberries, and wild orange, and tended the vegetables he grew in the garden plot.

Although Charlie had abandoned the old mode of dress in favor of dungarees, Lillie had not. Her thin body was covered to the ankles by the colorful long dress, and a multi-colored cape was always draped around her shoulders. Her hair was balled on top of her head and held fast by a hairnet, and the silver eardrops came down to meet a dozen strands of glass beads that she wore around her neck. She was extremely shy and quiet, and would not speak to a stranger even in reply to a question. It was seldom that she said more than a few necessary words even to her husband or son, and it was only the grandson, Timmy, who could make her laugh.

Charlie was joined in his fish-cleaning chore by a large raccoon that jumped onto his shoulder and started clawing his head frantically.

"You stop that now, Gumbo," he said. "Don't I always give you a piece of the fish? Can't you have patience? You will get your share."

He had kept the 'coon as a pet for many years, and it had the free run of the chickees. It often took its meals at the same table with them, sometimes eating from Charlie's bowl. A hunter had shot the animal's mother and left it lying on the ground where it had fallen, and Charlie had named the small one Gumbo because he had found it on the limb of a gumbo limbo tree. The 'coon kept scratching at Charlie's head until he handed it a strip of fish, which it turned over and over in its paws before it began to eat.

The old couple did not have any set meal times and ate only when hungry. There was always food cooking on the grate, and now the smell of a turtle stew made Charlie's nose twitch. He came over to the cooking chickee, put the cleaned bass in a pan, and dished himself up a bowl of the stew. Just as he started eating he heard the rattle of a vehicle coming along the gravel road. An old 1960 Ford pickup turned down the narrow trail leading to the clearing and stopped. Billy Joe Jumper got out of the truck and came over to the chickee, closely followed by Timmy.

"Hello, Pappa," Billy Joe said, taking a seat on one of the cabbage palm stumps used as chairs.

"You want to eat?" Charlie asked. "We have a fresh turtle stew."

"No thanks, Pappa. I'm not hungry."

"Will you take me fishing, Granpappa?" Timmy asked quickly. He always got excited when he came to the camp of his grandfather, for he loved to go into the swamp with the old man in the dugout canoe.

"It is up to your father," Charlie answered. "You must ask him first."

"I guess he can stay," Billy Joe said. "I've got to carry the rent money up to Immokalee. I came by to see if you need anything from the store."

"I need a bolt of the blue cloth and three spools of red thread," Lillie said. "I have the money here." She got up from the sewing machine, took a tin can from the overhead shelf, and handed a roll of bills to Billy Joe.

"Is that all you need?" he asked.

"We need a can of coffee and a sack of the plain flour," she said. "And I have one finished jacket you can sell."

"It won't bring as good a price in Immokalee as it would in Naples or down on the Trail. Keep it here and I will sell it for you later this week."

Billy Joe got up to leave, then he turned to Timmy and said, "You mind your grandfather, you hear? And don't pester your grandmother. And don't pull Gumbo's tail. I will come back for you this afternoon."

Billy Joe turned the pickup west on the narrow limestone road that led from the swamp to Turner River Grade, a gravel road that ran north through the Copeland Prairie to Alligator Alley, the Everglades Parkway toll highway. Instead of turning north when he reached the Grade, he turned west again on the state road to Copeland, where he would sell a hamper of tomatoes to the Janes Store. He did not want to take the tomatoes all the way to Immokalee because the intense heat would make them soft, and the price would not then be as good.

When he reached the store in Copeland, which was on Highway 29 three miles north of the Tamiami Trail, he sold the tomatoes and purchased the things his mother wanted. Just above Miles City the highway intersected Alligator Alley, and he stopped for a few minutes and watched the stream of speeding cars heading east and west across the two-lane toll road that connected Naples with Fort Lauderdale.

The hot May sun was causing heat waves to rise

from the asphalt, and because of the long drought there was little water in the drainage ditch that paralleled the highway. There had been no rain for almost eight months, and the fields and pastures were burned a deep brown. Even the fronds of the cabbage palms that bordered the highway seemed to be smoking.

When he reached Immokalee he went to the small concrete block building that housed the office of Riles Real Estate Agency. At a front desk he gave the rent money to a secretary, and while she was writing his receipt, Kenneth Riles came in. He was a young man of twenty-nine who had inherited the real estate business when his father died five years ago.

"How are things with you, Billy Joe?" Riles asked, handing a sheaf of papers to the secretary.

"Drought is beginning to hurt bad," Billy Joe said.

"Yes, it's sure bad. We really need some rain. And by the way, Billy Joe, I just received a notice that ten thousand acres of the land that belongs to the Potter Estate in Miami has been sold. That section includes the land where you live. I wouldn't think that the rent price would change, but if it does I'll let you know. Until we learn more about the plans of the new owner, just keep making the rent payments here the same as usual."

"I will, Mr. Riles. And if the rent goes up, I'd appreciate your letting me know right away."

Billy Joe then drove to the office of the Everglades Gazette, which was owned by Albert Lykes. Lykes was also an attorney although he practiced little law any more. He was in his late fifties and devoted most of his time to the small weekly newspaper.

When Billy Joe had purchased the pickup truck from a used car lot in Naples he had been overcharged two hundred dollars on the finance charges. When Lykes learned of this he had recovered Billy Joe's money and then refused to accept a fee for doing so. Lykes was known as a lawyer who would handle legal matters for the Seminoles at no cost, and he counted most of them in the area as his friends. Billy Joe always brought him something when he came to Immokalee.

Albert Lykes was sitting at a desk in his small cluttered office when Billy Joe entered. He did not look up from his work quickly, for in the jeans, faded blue denim shirt, boots, and cowboy hat, Billy Joe resembled any of dozens of other men to be seen on the streets and in the businesses of this cattle center. When he finally recognized who had entered he pushed the papers away and said cheerfully, "Well, hello, Billy Joe. Have a seat. How are things with you?"

"I brought you some beans and some okra," Billy Joe said, handing Lykes a brown paper bag. "It's not much, though. The drought has about ruined my whole vegetable crop."

"Yes, we're really beginning to hurt everywhere. The fires have already burned thousands of acres in the southern Glades, and some of the fires have burned down so deep into the muck that they say it will take years for them to burn out even after we get rain. What we need is a pure flood."

"I sure hope the fire doesn't break out in the swamp. I don't see how it could ever be stopped there." Billy Joe pulled up a chair, sat down and said, "Mr. Lykes, they just told me down at the real estate office that ten thousand acres of land out there where I live have been sold. Why would anybody buy that much land so far out in the swamp? Most of the cypress has already been cut a long time ago."

"Who told you that?" Lykes asked quickly.

"Mr. Riles. He said he didn't know if the rent would change or not, but he'd let me know as soon as he heard something. I sure hope it doesn't go up. After this drought killing my crop I'd have a real hard time getting up more money."

"I don't know why anyone would want that land, Billy Joe, unless they're just speculating. It's an awfully isolated place. If I can find out anything I'll let you know."

"I would sure appreciate it, Mr. Lykes. And you come see us. We'll take you fishing."

"Thanks for the vegetables," Lykes said, "and anytime you're in town, come by to see me."

As Billy Joe turned back down Highway 29 towards home he was troubled by the news of the sale of the land. He just didn't understand why anyone would want to buy it.

As soon as his father had left, Timmy dipped a bowl into the turtle stew and began to eat ravenously, although for breakfast that morning he had eaten hot biscuits, corn grits, and fried ham. His mother could not cook the wild game and the turtle as well as his grandmother, and he often slipped off and came down to the chickees to eat an extra meal. His grandmother made the corn bread in a five-inch deep loaf, and he broke off a chunk of the steaming-hot pone and dipped it into the juice of the stew. The turtle meat was sweet and tender, and he licked his fingers after each bite.

Charlie watched in silence for a few minutes, then he said, "You eat like a hungry panther. It is good for you. Make you grow big and strong."

Timmy had the same Seminole features as his father and his grandmother, the high cheekbones, the deep brown color, the slightly slanted, piercing eyes. But unlike his grandfather, his eyes were searching and excited rather than tired and squinting.

He finished the bowl of stew and said, "Are we going into the swamp now, Granpappa?"

"I have not finished my food. If you are in such a hurry, you go and dig the worms for the bait."

Timmy jumped up and ran to the storage chickee, took out a shovel, and headed for the area of the abandoned hog pen. He came back shortly with a can filled with worms and put them, along with two cane poles, into the dugout. The poles were equipped with lines the same length as the poles, turkey quills, and small hooks. Charlie used them only when fishing with Timmy for the bream, for when he hunted the black bass and the garfish, he used the spear.

As they started down Gopher Creek, Timmy sat in the front of the dugout and watched his grandfather move them swiftly across the water. He studied each stroke of the pole in his grandfather's hands. He had always been fascinated by each task Charlie performed, even the seemingly simple things like removing the shell from a turtle or cleaning a fish or carving a bowl from a block of cypress. He had a deep love for his grandfather and hoped that someday he could be like him.

He finally broke the silence and said, "Where are we going, Granpappa?"

"We will fish for the bream in the otter pond."

"Will you take me to the big tree?"

"We will go to the tree first and fish on the way back."

They moved quickly along a narrow winding stream bordered on both sides by growths of oak and willow and dwarf cypress and wax-myrtle, laced overhead by a dozen varieties of vines. The landscape then changed suddenly and they were in the open area of the dwarf cypress swamp where Charlie had turned right that morning on his way to the giant alligator. This time they went straight ahead, and on the far side of the clearing they found a stream that led back into a dense area of swamp.

After another mile this stream widened out and spread its black water across the entire land; and rising up before them, towering a hundred and fifty feet into the sky, was a giant bald cypress that had escaped the saw when the loggers had ravished the swamp several decades before.

Charlie poled the dugout close to the base of the tree, and when Timmy looked up it seemed to him that the trunk went out of sight into the clouds. Around the base of the tree, which must be at least fifty feet in circumference, the cypress knees grew so thick that the canoe could not pass through them.

Timmy said excitedly, "Can I climb it, Granpappa? Please let me climb it this time. You promised you would let me do it someday."

Years ago Charlie had built a ladder up the side of the tree, driving the rungs in one at a time with nails, moving slowly upward and driving in the cypress rungs until he had no more, then climbing down to the canoe and going back up with more rungs and more nails, moving steadily upward until finally he had reached the top where the limbs forked outward and upward in graceful curves. From the top he could see above all the other trees, across the roof of the swamp, past the point where the trees suddenly stopped and the great sea of sawgrass began, over the River of Grass dotted with the thick growths of the hammocks as far away to the horizon as the eye could see.

He thought for a moment and said to Timmy, "Not this time. You will climb it, but this is not the time. You must be strong, or your arms would give way before you reached the top."

"Can you see Forever Island from up there?" Timmy asked.

"No, you cannot see Forever Island. You can. see the way, but it is too far. It is many miles to the south."

"You will let me climb it someday, won't you, Granpappa?"

"Yes. I promise you, you will climb the tree."

Timmy sat back down in the bottom of the dugout and the old man poled them off in a westward direction. He left this swamp by a different stream and soon came to a pond dotted with dwarf cypress and pickerel weed. He stopped close to a clump of weeds and said, "We will try here for bream, but you must be very quiet. The bream will run away if they hear a sound."

Timmy put a worm on the hook, adjusted the turkey quill to a depth of two feet, then threw it out close to the weeds. As soon as the hook had sunk, the quill darted downward and the line became taut. Timmy pulled in a fat bream and dropped it into the dugout. Each time a hook hit the water the same thing happened, and soon they had boated more than a dozen fish.

Charlie wrapped his line back around the pole, dropped it onto the bottom of the dugout and said, "We will quit now. You have all the fish you can eat."

As Timmy wrapped his line around the pole, Charlie watched a heron pecking at minnows along the edge of the water. The flat was also being worked by wood ibis and water turkey. He pointed to a nearby mudbank and said, "You see the marks there. It is where the otter slides down into the water to play. They have been watching us catch their fish. Would you like to see them?"

Timmy finished wrapping the line and put it down. "Yes, Granpappa. Maybe we can catch one and I can carry it home with me."

"You will not catch the otter with your hands. He is

too fast. Only the alligator can catch the otter, and he cannot do it unless the otter's mind is elsewhere."

Charlie picked up one of the fish and threw it to the edge of the water. Almost instantly, a brown otter shot down the mudbank, grabbed the fish in its mouth, stared intensely at the man and boy, then scurried back up the bank. The otter paused for a moment more, again staring at the intruders, then he scurried out of sight into the brush.

"Sometimes they will come out and play for you," Charlie said. "They have even come into the chickees. If we stayed here longer, they would not be afraid. But we must go now. We have fish to clean for your supper."

Timmy lay on his back and looked upward into the trees and the sky as his grandfather poled the dugout toward home. It made him dizzy to watch the limbs and the vines and the clouds fly by overhead, and hear the rippling of the water as the ancient canoe sliced through the swamp. High up in the sky he could see a flight of white ibis winging its way south toward the marsh country, and, although he could not see it, he listened to the deep-throated croak of a great blue heron. He draped one leg over the side of the dugout and let the water swirl across his bare foot. In a moment he was asleep and was awakened only when he became aware that the movement of the dugout had stopped.

When Timmy pushed himself up he did not see his grandfather. For a moment he was startled, then he looked up a shallow slough and saw Charlie snatching something from the bottom and putting it into his pocket. He soon returned to the canoe and said, "Crawfish. They are for Gumbo. These are for him like candy is for you. He could eat a gallon if you would give it to him."

When they started to leave, Charlie suddenly stopped the dugout again and walked back up the slough. He noticed a fresh gash cut into the side of a tree, then he waded further up the slough. As far as he could see into the swamp there was a line of fresh gashes cut into trees. He wondered about this for a moment, then he turned and retraced his path back to Timmy.

As soon as the bow of the dugout touched land at the chickees, the 'coon jumped in and smelled the fish, then he climbed to Charlie's shoulder and started scratching his head. Charlie put him out of the dugout. "The fish are not for you, Gumbo," he said. "They are for Timmy. This is what I brought for you." When he took the crawfish from his pocket and dropped them on the ground, the 'coon let out a high-pitched yell, almost like a chuckle; then he grabbed one and turned it over and over in his paws.

Lillie was still at the sewing machine when Timmy scampered up the bank and to the chickee. "Can I have some more stew?" he asked eagerly.

"You can have what you wish," she said, smiling. "There is plenty. It is good for you to eat."

He dipped a bowl of the stew, broke off a large piece of corn pone, and again ate with relish.

TWO

SETH's FISH CAMP was two miles eastward on Gopher Creek from Charlie's chickees, and the narrow limestone road ended at the camp. The owner was Seth Thompson, who had been born on the campsite and had lived all of his sixty-five years there except for a period of time in his youth when he had been a commercial fisherman during the catfish boom at Lake Okeechobee.

Seth's father had bought the ten-acre homesite from a mail-order advertisement in 1890, had sold his small farm in Georgia, and headed south to Florida and the land of milk and honey which the advertisement guaranteed. It pictured tomatoes that weighed five pounds and okra two feet long and sugar cane twenty feet tall and soil so rich that, if you threw a stick on the ground, by the next day a tree would have sprouted.

John Thompson arrived south of Lake Okeechobee six months later with an ox cart filled with plows and axes and dreams, and the further south he traveled the deeper the water became and the more impenetrable the swamp. He finally abandoned the cart and the oxen and waded onto his property with only an axe and a rifle. For the next year he slept on the wet muck and swatted millions of mosquitoes while he built the small house from the stand of virgin bald cypress. He drew his bare living from the swamp and sold the pelts of the animals he killed for food.

Many times he thought of abandoning his property and seeking out the real estate company that had tricked and fleeced him, but he stayed and gradually hacked a small piece of the land from the jungle and grew a few six-ounce tomatoes and three-inch okra.

In 1906, while on a trip to Okeechobee City, he married the daughter of a fisherman and brought her back to the cypress house in the swamp. She stayed just long enough for Seth to be born, then she left man and child and swamp and was not seen again by John Thompson.

Seth and his embittered father had no father-son relationship, and his father looked upon him as something he could not swat dead only because of the law. He tolerated the boy for thirteen years, and then Seth ran away to Lake Okeechobee and secured work in the catfish industry.

Seth would occasionally come back home and give his father what money he could spare, and the relationship gradually warmed. It was during such a brief visit in 1931 that Seth found his father dead in the small tomato patch. He buried him in the cemetery at Copeland.

Seth came back to the property and brought with him a new bride from Moore Haven, and then he experienced the same thing as his father. One week in the dilapidated cypress house and the mosquito-infested swamp was enough, and on the eighth morning Seth awoke to find that his bride had vanished. Unlike his father, though, he was not embittered. She had been unable to cook and had refused to chop logs and skin animals, and it suited him that she was gone.

By this time the great catfishing boom at Lake Okeechobee had played out, and there was still much of a demand for fish, so Seth began commercial fishing in the creeks and sloughs of the swamp and in nearby Turner River. As he grew older and lost his taste for the long hard hours of commercial fishing, he added rental boats and sold his services as a guide, and gradually Seth's Fish Camp became known to the sportsfishermen of Collier County. He would now do commercial fishing only when he needed the money.

The old house was still as it had been when built in 1890, with the sagging front porch, thick plank floor and hand-hewn shingles. To the left of the house there was parked a Ford pickup truck and a swamp buggy with its huge airplane tires. Close to the creek Seth had built a shack that served as his store. Here he sold such items as fishing tackle, beer, soda pop, candy, and cigarettes, but he drank a great deal more of the beer than he sold. A dozen flat-bottomed rental boats were pulled onto the bank of the creek, and everywhere around the clearing there were piles of fish nets and traps.

The only modern conveniences added to the place were the electric lines, the cooler for the beer and soda pop, a refrigerator, and a big Coca-Cola sign across the front of the store that read Seth's Fish Camp. He still cooked his meals on an open grill in front of the house or on a wood-burning stove in the kitchen. There was an outdoor privy in the woods back of the house, and baths were taken in a wooden tub on the rear porch. He did, however, have an electric pump to draw water into the house and to the stand on the edge of the creek where fish were cleaned.

Seth had an assistant known only by the name of Slim, a gangling man of forty who had walked into the camp ten years ago and asked for a meal and had never left. Seth had never known where Slim had come from or where he was going or if he had any other name, and he had never asked. Slim became a faithful helper around the camp, ate little, and did whatever he was told to do without question, and this was enough for Seth. He lived in a room Seth had built for him on the back of the store, and it was obvious that he had no intention of ever leaving.

The one thing that distinguished Seth's place from any other part of the swamp was the nine acres of virgin bald cypress surrounding the camp. No timber had ever been cut except for the one acre where the earlier gardening venture had been tried, and those trees went into the building of the house and sheds. Now the somber trees reached high into the sky, with boughs so thick that no sunlight ever came through, and the ground was covered with cypress knees of all shapes and heights and tall graceful ferns and sphagnum moss. There were ponds filled with water lilies; thick growths of palmetto and wild orchids; and there

was a quietness that was almost unearthly. Many people came to the camp just to walk through these woods.

Seth Thompson at sixty-five was a rotund man, five feet eleven in height and carrying two hundred and eighty pounds, a modern-day Falstaff, always smiling, dressed only in a pair of faded overalls. Even when he made trips into Naples or Everglades City or Fort Myers or Immokalee to sell fish or buy supplies he donned neither shirt nor shoes, and if he had, he would not have been recognized by those who had known him for many years. He was accepted for what he was, both by those who came to his camp and by those who came into contact with him in the towns and cities, and he was no more of a curiosity than any other of the white men or Indians who made the Big Cypress their home.

Seth was daubing tar on the bottom of a rental boat when Charlie pushed the bow of the dugout onto the bank. He always stopped by to visit with Seth when on this part of the creek. As soon as the canoe touched land, Gumbo jumped out and started shaking a gourd rattle. Charlie sometimes took Gumbo with him on the shorter trips into the swamp, and the 'coon would run up and down the dugout, shaking the rattle to frighten the birds. Charlie had made it for him from a dried gourd and little limestone pebbles. But he never took Gumbo with him when he went to feed Little George, for he knew if the 'coon jumped out of the dugout, he would make one good bite for the giant alligator.

Seth looked up and said, "Well howdy, Charlie. How about a beer?"

He always offered the old Seminole a beer, and Charlie sometimes accepted. He relished the taste of the cold brew, but he seldom drank more than one for fear that his head would swim.

Seth put down the tar pot, looked toward the shack and shouted, "Slim, git on out here and bring us a couple of brews."

The lanky man sauntered from the store with two cans of beer. He was dressed the same as Seth except that he wore an oversize pair of brogan shoes. He handed the cans to Seth and said, "Howdy, Charlie. How's yore folks?"

"They are fine," Charlie replied, taking one of the cans from Seth. Slim turned and went back into the store.

Both men got up and moved into the shade of a moss-festooned oak whose limbs nearly covered the house. They squatted on their haunches and faced each other, Seth's huge stomach bulging out so far that he could not see his feet. Charlie took a drink of the beer and said, "It is good. It makes my stomach chuckle."

Gumbo ran up and snatched at the can, and Seth said, "Give him a little snort, Charlie. It won't hurt him none."

Charlie held the can down while the 'coon put his mouth to the rim and sucked. Then Gumbo jumped back, scratched, twitched his nose, and scampered onto the seat of the swamp buggy.

"Guess he's going to take a little ride now that he's likkered up," Seth laughed. He took a deep drink from the can. "Shore mighty hot and dry. They's places I can't even get into anymore in a boat. Water's down two feet and more, and in some of them little ponds they ain't but a few inches left. We need a regular flood of rain."

"Are you fishing now?" Charlie asked.

"Ah, I'm doin' a little, catchin' some catfish and some mullet over in Turner River. Ain't many fishermen comin' out here now and rentin' boats with the water so low and it so hot and dry. So's I thought I might as well sell a few for pocket money whiles I'm not doin' too much around the camp."

"I saw a strange thing this morning," Charlie said, suddenly changing the subject. "There is a slough southeast of here, about five miles, where the birds feed, and I went there to cut some small pond cypress. There were two ducks that were dead, and a spoonbill that could not move itself, and it died too while I was there. They were young birds, and they had not been shot."

"Well, I guess even the critters can get sick and die before their time. I've seen dead birds before in the swamp. Could be something they et."

"Maybe so."

Seth sucked the last drop of beer from the can. "You ready for another?" he asked.

"This is enough. This one was good, but if I have another I might point the dugout toward Cape Sable instead of home."

"Ah, you better have another. A man can't travel on one leg, you know."

"Thank you, but I must go now."

Seth got up and followed Charlie down to the creek bank. "What you going to do with them small logs?" he asked.

"I am going to hew out the little dugout canoes to be sold to the tourist places on the Tamiami Trail."

"How come?" Seth said, laughing and digging his elbow into Charlie's side. "You ain't got a woman somewheres that's hittin' you up for money, have you?"

"No woman would want even money from such an old dog as me," Charlie said. "Lucy, the daughter of Billy Joe, is going to marry Frank Willie, and Billy Joe wants to give them the television for a present. He has lost his crop to the drought, and he is worried that he cannot now do this. So I will help, and Lillie will help, and we will not tell Billy Joe until we have earned the money. The little canoes will bring a fair price."

"Shoot, if that's all that's botherin' you, I'll help too. Me and you can gather some cypress knees, 'cause they bring a good price too, and I know a place down in Miami that'll buy all the snake hides you can get, and we can get some frogs and sell the legs. Shoot, them frog legs is high as a cat's back now. I ain't doin' much of nothin' around here now, so I'll help. You just let me know when you want to get started."

"It is kind of you to offer, Seth. I will let you know. And I thank you for the beer." He turned to leave, then he stopped and said, "Have you been marking a trail on the trees anywhere in the swamp?"

"What you mean, Charlie?" Seth asked, puzzled.

"Cutting gashes on the trees with a hatchet."

"Shoot, no. I got better things to do than that. How come you ask?"

"It is nothing, I guess. I saw such a fresh trail the other day, but maybe it was a hunter who feared losing his way."

"Ain't no hunters out here this time of year and you know it," Seth said. "But I don't know what kind of a fool would go around choppin' on trees."

Charlie then put Gumbo into the dugout and pushed the slim craft out into the creek. "We will see you again soon, Seth," he said.

"You come back anytime, Charlie. And you just let me know when you want to get started raisin' that money for the television."

THREE

CHARLIE WAS SITTING on the ground striking chips from a miniature dugout when he heard the sound of an airboat coming down the creek. He put the work aside and watched as the craft came around the bend and approached the chickees. It was Fred Henderson, the game warden. He cut the engine and guided the bow of the boat onto the landing.

Henderson was a youthful looking man of thirty-five who had worked this area of the county for the past nine years. Six years ago he had been shot by alligator poachers, but this had been before the law was strengthened, making alligator poaching a felony punishable by up to five years in prison. This new and more drastic law, combined with a vanishing market for hides, had made poaching almost a thing of the past, although a few alligators were still killed or captured illegally. But it would never again be the booming business it once was, and now the wardens could spend more time enforcing the game and fish laws.

Fred Henderson stepped from the boat and said, "Hi there, Mr. Charlie." He always visited this camp when traveling the area of Gopher Creek.

"Hi there, Fred Henderson. You want tea?"

"Sure," the warden smiled. "I came twenty miles out of the way to get a mug of that special brew of yours."

Charlie got up, went to the cooking chickee, and returned with two steaming mugs of a dark colored brew.

Henderson took a sip. "Man, that's good. Really makes your motor run."

"It is the secret Black Drink," Charlie said. "It cleans out a man's innards. It is good for you." Charlie then chuckled, for it was only harmless sassafras and not the legendary Black Drink used during the Green Corn Dance festival to purge all the males.

"Well, if it's what you say, I better give it back, 'cause I've got a long ride ahead of me out in the sawgrass, and you know what would happen if I hung my bottom over the side of the boat and some of that sharp sawgrass got ahold of me." Henderson then laughed also, for he knew exactly what was in the brew.

Charlie said, "Only the Seminole knows how to do his business in the sawgrass and come away without injury."

"I can believe that," Henderson said. He looked about the clearing and asked, "Where's Gumbo?"

"He is right above you."

The warden looked up and the 'coon was coming down an oak limb, just about ready to pounce upon him. One leap and Gumbo straddled his shoulders.

"Man, you've gotten fat, Gumbo," Henderson said, taking the 'coon from his shoulders.

"He eats only ten meals each day," Charlie said.

"Well, you better watch him. Some big 'gator sure would like to have him for a meal." The warden finished the drink and got up. "You want to ride with me? I'll bring you back in a couple of hours."

"Yes, I will go," Charlie beamed, for one of his greatest pleasures was riding in the swift airboat.

Charlie was still grinning when the engine thundered to life and the craft moved off slowly down Gopher Creek. They made their way through the shallow ponds and the sloughs and then into the vast River of Grass, the open Glades that stretched southward all the way to Cape Sable and to Florida Bay.

When they reached the open marsh the boat picked up speed and crashed through the razor-sharp sawgrass, which was sometimes as high as ten feet and sometimes only two feet. Dotted over the landscape there were hammocks filled with cabbage palm, oak, lancewood, poisonwood, gumbo limbo, all interlaced with vines.

Sometimes the warden guided the boat along open paths through the sawgrass which were mostly trails wallowed out by alligators; and sometimes they would break through a wall of grass and suddenly come into small ponds filled with water lilies. Here the alligator eyes peeked up at them out of lily pads. Ahead of them the coots and the ducks scurried out of the way, and once they surprised a little coot that went under the boat and came out behind them uninjured but with a ruffled pride.

They made a wide circle through the marsh and

then turned back north. They could see just how much the towering royal palms overshadowed the other trees. Their slick trunks rose upward for a hundred and seventy-five feet and their green down-turned tops resembled tiny umbrellas above the roof of the swamp. From this distance it seemed that the swamp's mixture of trees formed a solid wall that could not be penetrated, but as they drew closer, many openings came into view.

When they entered the swamp, Charlie signaled for Henderson to stop. He idled the motor and Charlie said, "Have you been by Muscadine Slough?"

"Not in a good while," Henderson replied, "but I know where it is."

"I saw several dead birds there yesterday. They were young, and they had not been shot."

"Well, let's take a quick look. Can we get there with the airboat?"

"The water is low, but I went there in the dugout. I do not believe the airboat will have trouble."

They moved very slowly, Henderson guiding the boat around decayed logs and fallen limbs, following narrow paths when he could, sometimes gunning the powerful engine and shooting over the shelves of shallow mudbanks, pushing through beds of the deadly cottonmouths and making the snakes run from the thunder of the engine.

The east end of the slough was narrow, but as it turned a bend it widened and formed a pond of about ten acres. The water level was down from a normal four feet to a scant six inches, and there was no water movement in or out of the area, making the entire pond stagnant. Birds scattered into the swamp at the approach of the airboat.

Henderson came into the main pond, cut the engine and looked about. "Good God," he exclaimed in puzzlement, "what has happened here?"

There were dead birds lying everywhere: Florida mallard, ringnecks, blue-winged teal, coots, black-necked stilts, white ibis, American egrets, grebe, gallinule, gull-billed terns, Louisiana heron, skimmers, glossy ibis, and roseate spoonbills. Many others were paralyzed, not yet dead but unable to move, their wings outspread and their beaks turned upward, struggling to move.

Henderson just sat and stared silently until Charlie said, "It was not this bad yesterday. There were only three."

"It must be getting every bird that stops by this pond. I've never seen anything like this. Dead birds, yes. But not this."

The warden took two metal containers and scooped them down into the water and the muck, then he sealed them and put them aside. "I'll move around the edges and you pick up about a dozen of the dead ones," he said to Charlie. "As soon as we get back I'll rush them and the water samples to the lab. They can probably figure it out pretty fast."

After they had gathered the dead birds, Henderson pushed the airboat through the swamp and toward Gopher Creek. He moved faster now, and he and Charlie had no more jokes nor conversation. Charlie got out at his landing and the airboat shot away up the creek.

FOUR

TIMMY HAD RUN DOWN the dirt lane to the chickees early the next morning, and Charlie was just finishing a breakfast of biscuits baked in the dutch oven, hot corn grits, and slices of fried turtle meat. He was pouring a mug of coffee as Lillie busied herself preparing a pot of fish chowder.

Even before he said "Can I have one?" Timmy had grabbed a hot biscuit, broken it in half, stuffed it with crisp turtle meat, and plopped it into his mouth. Between munches he said, "Can we go into the swamp this morning, Granpappa?"

"I must go to the camp of Seth Thompson, and then I have work to do, but you can go with me to the camp, and maybe we can come back through the swamp."

Timmy heard a rattling sound and looked up, and Gumbo was on top of the chickee, shaking the gourd. "Do not pay him any mind," Charlie said. "He has eaten twice already this morning. He is worse than a hog. Now he is just wanting your attention."

When Charlie finished his coffee, they got into the dugout and started up the creek. This time Timmy sat in the furthest point of the bow, looking ahead and skimming his hands through the cool water. It did not take the sleek craft but a short time to move the two miles to the fish camp.

Seth was inside the store when they arrived, and he came out with a can of beer in his hand. He greeted Charlie in the usual way, "How about a can of beer?"

"Not this time, Seth. It is too early in the morning for me. I thank you anyway."

Timmy ran across the clearing, jumped onto the swamp buggy, grabbed the steering wheel, and made sounds like the motor running. Charlie squatted down and said to Seth, "When are you going down by the Trail again?"

Seth plopped down in front of him, his huge stomach almost touching the ground. "I got to make a trip down to Everglades City tomorrow morning. You need something?"

"I have one of the little canoes finished. Billy Joe could sell it for me, but I don't want him to know of this until we have our share for the television. And Lillie has two jackets."

"Shore, I'll take 'um down with me. How much you want for the canoe?"

"I do not know. What do you think?"

"Well, I've seen them things sell to the tourist for about thirty dollars, so you ought to get fifteen. I'll do the best I can. I ain't no fool when it comes to dealing with them crooks down on the Trail."

"We will have the things ready when you come by."

"Shoot, long as I'm makin' a haul for you anyway,

why don't we go out tonight and get a mess of them frog legs. I could sell 'um to the Rod and Gun Club down in Everglades City. Some folks pays as much as two or three dollars for a plate of them things, and they ought to bring at least sixty cents a pound, maybe more."

"We will go if you have the time."

"I got the time, Charlie. 'Bout all I've got ever night is time. I'll pick you up sometime after dark."

The sound of an airboat stopped the conversation, and Fred Henderson turned in to the camp when he saw Charlie and Seth together. He cut the engine and got out.

"How about a beer, Fred?" Seth asked.

"Thanks, but no thanks," the warden replied.

Seth and Charlie both got up, and Henderson said to Charlie, "Got a call early this morning from the lab down in West Palm. It's a bacteria killing those birds. They said that when the water gets real low, this bacteria can multiply and really do some damage. It'll take rising water to stop it. They told us to go in there and burn all the dead birds and try to keep the others away from that area. We've got a man who's going to stay in there and fire a shotgun to scare the birds off. The bacteria might be in just that one pond, so the important thing is to keep the birds out of there. Beyond that, they say there's nothing we can do, except maybe pray for rain."

"Is that the place you told me about, Charlie?" Seth asked.

"Yes. It is the east end of Muscadine Slough. I went

by there again yesterday with Fred, and we found many dead birds, maybe eighty or a hundred. And others were sick."

"If either of you run across this somewhere else, please let me know right away," Henderson said. "I'll be running this area for the next few days. And we sure thank you, Mr. Charlie, for pointing this thing out. Something like this could happen out in the swamp and we wouldn't know about it until it's too late to do anything."

As soon as Henderson was gone, Charlie and Timmy got into the dugout and started back down the creek. About halfway home Charlie stopped the canoe and said to Timmy, "Look very close there in the mudbank."

Timmy peered into the water and could see that a large snapper turtle had buried itself in the mud with only its head showing. Its mouth was open, and two appendages inside its mouth were waving gently in the slow moving current.

Charlie said, "Little fish will think those are worms."

Timmy continued to watch as a small bream slowly approached the waving tentacles, then it suddenly darted to them. The turtle's mouth snapped shut.

"The turtle has now had his dinner," Charlie said. "I will come back sometime and take the turtle for my dinner. It is the way of all things in the swamp. We all depend on each other."

Timmy frowned for a moment, then he said, "It

seemed like a bad trick, Granpappa. The little fish did not know better."

As Charlie pushed the canoe away and continued downstream, he repeated, "It is the way of all things, Timmy."

When the evening meal was finished, Charlie and Lillie sat around the flickering fire in the cooking chickee. From far in the south a rumble of dry thunder echoed through the swamp. Lillie was rocking back and forth gently, her hands in her lap, looking as if she were half asleep.

She turned to Charlie and said, "Why do we not have the electric line brought to the chickee? It passes here on the way to the fish camp."

At first Charlie didn't know what to say in reply, for she had never mentioned this before. For a few moments he remained silent.

She spoke again, "If we had the electric line I could be sewing now. My eyes cannot see by the firelight anymore."

He finally said, "It would cost money each month. Billy Joe has to pay the first of each month."

"It would not be much. We could pay it from the things we sell. And later we could buy the electric box to make ice and to keep the meat and the fish from spoiling."

"Then we could keep the cans of cold Coca-Cola like Billy Joe, couldn't we?" For a moment he became silent as if in deep thought, then he said quickly, "We will do it! I will speak to Billy Joe and have him make the arrangements for us."

Just then Seth came out of the darkness of the creek and rammed the bow of his boat onto the landing. He walked to the chickee and eased himself slowly onto one of the palm stump seats.

"We have just decided to have the electric line brought to the chickee!" Charlie said triumphantly.

"You ought to have done it long before now," Seth said. "I've seen them chickees all up and down the Trail with electric lines runnin' to them. Ain't no sense you sittin' here in the dark ever night."

"And we will later buy the electric box to keep the fish and the meat and the cans of Coca-Cola."

"Shoot, you can pick them things up mighty cheap second hand. I don't see how folks nowdays gets along without a refrigerator. I know we used to, but I swear I don't know how we did it in all this heat. The fish and the meat won't keep no time without one. And besides that, it's mightly fine for beer."

"Do you think it is time for us to go?" Charlie asked.

"Well, they ain't no hurry, but we could mosey on into the swamp. It'll be a while yet afore them big frogs gets to stirrin' good. It wouldn't hurt, though, to get there a mite early and be ready for 'um."

Charlie went to the storage chickee and returned with his gig. Seth got up and said, "Miz Lillie, I got a cooler of cold beer down there in the boat if you would care for one."

"I thank you, but I do not believe so," Lillie said.

"Beer is for the men only. It does not seem right for a woman to belch loudly, and I have seen and heard what you men do when you drink the beer."

"Well, I guess you're right," Seth said, thinking that this was the longest speech he had ever heard Lillie make. "We'll see you a little later on."

Seth sat in the back of the boat and Charlie in the front, Seth guiding with a paddle and Charlie leading the way with a flashlight Seth had brought. There was also a gasoline lantern in the boat but they would not light it until they started the gigging. An outboard engine on the stern had been pulled out of the water and locked into position.

As they moved slowly into the outer edges of the swamp Charlie was riding two feet above Seth, for Seth's weight, plus the weight of the motor, had sunk the rear of the boat to within two inches of the water and shot the bow high into the air.

Seth reached into the cooler, took out two beers, opened them and handed one to Charlie. "Man can't travel on one leg on a dark night like this," he said.

The moon had not come up yet and the sky was covered with a thick cloud formation, and there were still rumbles of thunder coming from the south. The beam of the flashlight cut through the darkness like a drill, illuminating only a ten-foot-wide area at its furthest point.

The day creatures were now silent and the swamp was echoing the sounds of the night creatures: the chilling cry of the limpkin, the shrill squawk of the night heron, the fluttering wings of the night hawk in pursuit of mosquitoes, the gentle call of the hoot owl, and the terrifying scream of the screech owl. The alligators were beginning to bellow, and this, combined with the distinctive croaks of the bull frogs and the tree frogs, made a symphony of mis-matched melodies.

Seth stopped the boat momentarily and said, "Where you think we ought to go, Charlie? This boat don't draw much water, but my big butt's got her down by the stern. I'd shore hate to get stuck in a mudbank and have to wade out of here with them 'gators chasin' cottonmouths all over the place."

"The deepest place would be the pond just to the east of the big cypress. There is two feet and more of water there, and that pond has always been a good place for frogs."

"Well, from the sound of it they's plenty of frogs right here in the creek. But we'll start in the pond and work our way back." Seth threw the empty can onto the bottom of the boat and took another beer from the cooler. "You ready for another yet?" he asked.

"No. Too much beer would make me pee in my britches."

"Shoot, if that's your only problem, have another. You can always hang it over the side of the boat and let go. Who's going to see you out here in the swamp in black dark?"

"The alligator might see me and think it was a snake. Then I would be in great trouble."

"At your age that wouldn't matter none either. But I shore ain't got your problem. I got a set of kidneys

what can hold five gallons. You decide you want another one, it's right there in the cooler."

As they left the creek and turned right, Seth had to
dig the paddle into the muck and push them over an
area of shallow water. When they reached the outer
edge of the pond Charlie turned off the flashlight and
they were immediately immersed in a sea of total darkness. Not one beam of light drifted down from the sky,
and Seth could not even see the lantern sitting at his
feet. He found it with his hands, put a match to the
wick, and an orange flame sprang forth and put a globe
of dim light about the boat.

Charlie put the lantern in the bow of the boat, and
Seth moved them slowly around the edges of the pond.
The frogs were croaking everywhere, and in each area
the light touched, the yellowish glint of eyes came
from behind every lily pad and from each foot of mudbank. Charlie stood up and gigged the frogs, then
passed them back for Seth to take off the gig prongs.
Seth was in semidarkness and sometimes had to feel for
the frogs with his hands.

Within a half hour they had boated more than a
hundred frogs and had covered but a small portion of
the area. When Charlie passed one back, a loud clam-
oring and commotion started and the boat rocked so
violently that it almost threw him from his feet and
into the water. Seth shouted, "Charlie, you durn idiot,
get that thing out of here! It's a cottonmouth, not a
frog!" Seth had already grabbed the deadly snake before he realized what it was.

Charlie jerked the pole upward and flicked the snake high into the air away from the boat. " 'Gator will get him now," he said casually.

"Well, something sides a 'gator's goin' to get you, you do that again," Seth said, breathing heavily. "I durn near loaded my pants. Yore eyes ain't that old you can't tell a snake from a frog!"

"I knew it was a snake," Charlie chuckled. "I just wanted to see if you were awake."

"I'm durn sure awake now, so's you cut that out!" Seth sighed and said, "Gawd, that calls for a beer." He reached into the cooler, opened a can, drained it dry in one gulp, and opened another. "Let's rest a spell afore we go on."

Charlie sat down on the front seat, and they listened for a few moments as two wildcats started a screaming war dance against each other somewhere close by in the darkness. Seth finished the beer and they moved on, working the south side of the pond. Then they recrossed the swamp shallows and searched the banks of the creek on the way back to the chickees. It was after midnight when they reached the landing.

Charlie put the lantern on the bank and they cleaned the frogs, throwing the bodies into the water for the fish and snakes to eat. They had more than four hundred. Seth put the cleaned legs into the cooler to take back to his camp and keep in the refrigerator before taking them with him the next morning.

Seth put the engine back down into the water, started it, and moved off slowly up the creek. Charlie stood on the landing and watched until the lantern light moved around a bend and disappeared. The fire in the cooking chickee had burned down to gray embers as he walked stiffly toward his bed.

It was noon when Seth's old truck rambled down the path and stopped by the cooking chickee. Charlie was sitting on the ground, starting another little dugout, and Lillie was at the cooking fire. Seth got out and said, "Did pretty good for you folks." Charlie got up and came to the truck.

Seth took the money from his pocket and handed it to Charlie. He grinned and said, "Got fifteen dollars for the canoe and ten dollars apiece for the two jackets. We had forty-one pounds of dressed legs, and they brought 75¢ a pound. That made $30.75 for the lot. With the other stuff, you got $65.75 total."

"Did you take out your share of the legs?" Charlie asked.

"Naw, I didn't want nothin' out of it. It was fun to me, excep'in' when you flung that snake in my lap. We'll do it again any night you want to."

Charlie gave the money to Lillie, and she put it in a tin can on the shelf.

"Got something else, too," Seth said, grinning even more broadly. "Friend of mine who runs a store in Naples gave me this here old refrigerator to get it out of the way 'cause it looks so bad he couldn't sell it. Shore don't look like much, but it runs good. Thought you might like to have it for when your electric line comes in."

"You mean it did not cost anything?" Charlie asked.

"Naw. Them old things won't bring nothin' any-more. Anybody wants one, they get a new one. But this one will do you fine as new, if you don't mind the paint being gone. Help me get it off the truck."

Seth had bought the refrigerator for twenty-five dollars from an appliance dealer, but he knew Charlie wouldn't accept it if he told him this.

Lillie smiled as they took the old refrigerator from the truck and placed it beside the sewing platform in the chickee. She opened the door, closed it, then opened it again. "It's even cool without the electric line," she said. "I can store things in it until we can make it run."

"We sure thank you, Seth," Charlie said, as proud of the old refrigerator as he would have been with a new one. "Will you eat now?"

Lillie had cut sweet potatoes into thick slices, dipped them in flour and fried them along with a chicken, and there was still a pot of fish stew and a fresh pone of corn bread.

Seth looked at the food on the grill, then he sniffed deeply and sighed, "Don't mind if I do." He sat at the log table as Lillie heaped a plate and handed it to him.

Several days later, on his next visit to Little George, Charlie could hear the dull booms far in the east where the warden was firing a shotgun to frighten the birds away from Muscadine Slough. It reminded him of the days when the white men had come into the Glades to slaughter the snowy egret for its feathers, only this time the gun was firing in an effort to save the birds.

The constant sound disturbed him and sent fear through him, for it brought back memories of a time he hoped would never return. He did not linger after feeding the alligator, and on his return he poled the dugout swiftly so that he could get beyond the range of the sound. When he reached the south end of the creek he again noticed fresh gashes on a line of trees leading eastward into the swamp. He started to investigate this, but decided to push on to the chickees.

Late that afternoon Fred Henderson came by and informed Charlie that the firing would stop. The wardens in this area had been told by the district office in West Palm that they might be frightening infected birds into other parts of the swamp and marsh, thus possibly spreading the deadly bacteria instead of containing it. Their new orders were to continue burning the birds as they died in the Muscadine Slough area and to let what was happening run its course. There was nothing more that could be done, and only rising water could dissipate the bacteria and end this strange carnage.

FIVE

IT WAS THE MIDDLE of the following week when Kenneth Riles left his real estate office and came into the office of the Everglades Gazette. Albert Lykes was sitting at his desk, reading proof for the next issue of the newspaper. He looked up and motioned for Riles to take a seat.

Riles remained silent while Lykes finished reading a column of proof, then Lykes pushed the copy aside. "What can I do for you, Ken?" he asked.

"I've got a story for this week's edition," Riles said, his voice excited.

"What's that?"

"I've received notice that the ten thousand acres of Potter land out in Big Cypress that has changed hands has been purchased by Surf Development Corporation, and they're going to turn it into a new development with houses, condominiums, a recreational complex with a golf course—the whole works! It'll be called Everglades Villas. Al, we're going to have a real boom here in Collier County. With the twenty thousand acres already under development by Trans-Pacific, this will make thirty thousand acres under development at one time. If this keeps up we'll soon be as big as the Fort Lauderdale and Miami area."

Lykes leaned back in his chair. He had suspected this, but its confirmation still came as a shock. He finally said gruffly, "That boom you're talking about is going to be the Everglades exploding. Don't you know what this really means?"

Riles said emphatically, "It means more people and more jobs and more businesses and more tax money for the county and more money in circulation. It means progress."

For a moment Lykes just shook his head, then he said, "It means more drainage canals and more streets and more garbage to dump somewhere and more sewers flowing south and more animals retreating. Is that what you call progress?"

Riles was shocked and annoyed by Lykes' attitude. He said harshly, "Hell, Al, it's only a swamp, and there's plenty more swamp left!"

"Is there really?" Lykes asked. "It was twenty thousand acres yesterday and ten thousand today and maybe another thirty thousand gone tomorrow. When is it going to stop, Ken, when there's nothing left?"

"Well, what about the National Park?" Riles asked, the excitement now gone from his face. "Isn't that enough just for people to look at?"

"What good will there be in a park where nothing grows and no animals can live. Who would want to see that? If Big Cypress dies, the park dies. And that's a fact."

Riles got up from the chair. "I didn't come in here to argue, Al. I just thought you might be interested. But from your attitude I'd say you have a closed mind and that you're against this project regardless, just like you were dead set against the Trans-Pacific project and against the construction of Alligator Alley. You've just got a negative attitude all the way."

Lykes leaned forward and said, "Oh, I'm interested all right, Ken. But let me ask you one question. Are you going to be connected with this Surf project?"

"Yes," Riles said defensively. "I've been given a contract as one of the sales representatives."

"That's what I thought," Lykes said sadly.

"My being connected with the Surf project doesn't have anything to do with it. I'm for anything that brings progress to the county. As I said, though, I didn't come here to argue," Riles went on, his voice calmer. "If you want any more details on this project I'll be in my office."

As Riles started to leave, Lykes said, "Do Billy Joe Jumper and those other people who live out there have any idea of this yet?"

"No. I'll get around to telling them as soon as I can."

"I don't envy you that task," Lykes said, leaning back in the chair.

"Well, I'm sure when they moved onto land they didn't own they knew it wouldn't last forever."

"I guess you're right on that point. Nothing seems to last forever anymore."

For several minutes after Riles was gone, Lykes remained motionless in his chair, thinking back to the time when this development business first started. He was old enough to remember what the country once

looked like from Big Cypress to Lake Okeechobee
when most of the area was undeveloped and was the
natural watershed for Big Cypress and the Everglades.
He thought of the lush tropical growths and the clear
lakes and springs and the woods teeming with animals
and birds. Then came the drainage canals to trap the
water and carry it off to the Gulf on the west and the
Atlantic on the east, stopping this natural flow that was
the lifeblood for hundreds of square miles to the south;
and then the dike around Lake Okeechobee so that no
more water flowed south; and then more and more
drainage canals, more and more dikes, then the thousands and thousands of vegetable fields, each surrounded by a small dike and a drainage ditch; and
when the rain came it flowed from the fields and into
the drainage ditches, carrying with it the pesticides
and the fertilizer, the phosphates and the overflow
from thousands and thousands of septic tanks, seeping
slowly into the drainage canals and poisioning the
land. Great areas of the drained land became bone dry,
and the marshland muck dried up layer by layer and
blew away, leaving only bare limestone rock; and the
muck fires raged over hundreds of thousands of acres,
some burning downward for years, ruining the land as
a home for the birds and the animals and the reptiles
and the men who tried to live there; and then came
more land developers with their concrete block houses
and St. Augustine lawns, moving northward from
Homestead, westward from Miami and Hollywood and
Fort Lauderdale and West Palm Beach, draining and
building right out into the River of Grass, moving east-

ward from Fort Myers and Naples, and now it was
coming from north of the swamp.

Lykes suddenly leaned forward and reached for a
sheaf of clean paper. He knew that the only thing he
could do to fight the Surf project was to try to sway
public opinion against it through the editorial voice of
his small newspaper. This effort might be useless, but
at least he would try. He put a sheet of paper into his
battered old typewriter.

SIX

MAY PASSED INTO JUNE and still there was no rain. A fire had broken out in the woods adjoining Alligator Alley just sixteen miles north of the east end of Gopher Creek, and it had been brought under control only after Forest Service rangers from over the state had fought it for three days. Smoke from the smoldering trees, stumps, and muck was still drifting through the swamp.

Billy Joe had gotten a job cutting bushes and grass along Highway 29, and this prevented Timmy from coming to the chickees as much as he had previously. He now had the task of feeding the chickens and hogs and watering the few vegetable plants that were being nurtured for home consumption. The other plants in the field had wilted to the ground and were dead.

Seth and Charlie had made three more trips into the swamp at night gigging frogs, and the proceeds from this, along with the extra jackets Lillie had made and the canoes Charlie had carved, had pushed the secret television fund to a hundred and eighty dollars. Charlie thought if they could get two hundred and fifty dollars it would be a fair share of the cost and not place too much of a burden on Billy Joe, especially since the vegetable crop was now a total loss.

Seth and Charlie had planned another money making venture for that afternoon, a trip into the east swamp to gather cypress knees, but that morning Charlie had to cut more cypress for the little canoes. He had promised Timmy he could go with him, and now he was waiting for Timmy to finish his morning chores before coming to the chickees.

The refrigerator Seth had brought was still standing beside the sewing platform without power. Billy Joe had contacted the power company from the telephone in the Janes Store in Copeland and had been told, since there were no crews working in the Copeland area at the time, it might be two or three weeks before a crew could be sent in to run the line from the road to the chickee. This news did not disturb Charlie or Lillie. They had gotten along fine without the electricity for many decades, and a few weeks more would make no difference.

Timmy finally came trotting down the dirt trail and went to the landing where his grandfather was waiting. Charlie put the axe into the canoe and then pushed them away from the bank.

Charlie had decided to go to a different place this time to gather his logs in order to follow the deepest sloughs, for the water level had dropped even more. When he reached the area where the creek widened out into the swamp he turned left and went far to the south of Muscadine Slough. He had never before taken Timmy into this part of the swamp, and each passing

pond or island of button bush and pickerel weed was a
new adventure for Timmy.

They came to a small glade of higher ground and
Charlie stopped the dugout. The ground was covered
with lush ferns and a carpet of velvety green moss so
thick that their bare feet sank into it as they walked. A
giant live oak was entwined by a strangler fig that had
sent its runners upward through the limbs. The vine
would eventually kill the majestic tree and bring it
crashing to the ground.

Timmy suddenly stopped and said, "Granpappa, I
smell skunk. We better turn and run."

Charlie chuckled and said, "It is not skunk, Timmy.
It is the stopper tree. When the wind blows toward
you the tree gives off the odor of a skunk, but the smell
will not cling like the skunk. Maybe the tree wants us
to go away and not bother it."

They crossed the glade and waded out into a small
shallow pond filled with the dwarf cypress, where
Charlie cut three with the axe and brought them back
to the dugout. Then they headed south again, moving
close to the line where the swamp ends and the great
sawgrass marsh begins.

Charlie stopped again and said to Timmy, "Here I
will show you a thing you have not seen."

They walked into an area dotted with huge royal
palms, their stark trunks soaring above the roof of the
swamp. Charlie led Timmy to one tree so old that its
foilage was gone and its dead trunk riddled with holes
drilled by woodpeckers. The center of the bottom of
the trunk had encased an ancient machete, and al-

though the wooden handle was black with decay, the rust-covered blade was still solid.

Timmy immediately grabbed the handle and tried to pull the blade free, but it had long before become a part of the trunk.

"Where did it come from?" he asked excitedly.

"I do not know," Charlie said. "I found it here many years ago when I was a boy, and it had grown into the tree even then. Perhaps it has been here since the days of the first Seminole war. Someone, maybe a white soldier or an explorer, tried to chop down the tree and could not pull the blade out again."

"Can I have it, Granpappa?" Timmy asked. "We can chop the trunk away from it with the axe and I will carry it home with me."

"Let the tree that took it from the man keep it. It belongs to the tree."

"But the tree is dead, Granpappa."

"And so is the man. Let it stay here, Timmy. It is part of a time that will be no more."

Timmy agreed reluctantly and they walked to the dugout and headed back toward Gopher Creek.

Early that afternoon Charlie poled the dugout up the creek to meet Seth for the trip to gather cypress knees. Seth had said he knew a part of the swamp where there was a small stand of bald cypress remaining, and the knees there were plentiful. There were many knees on his land but he did not want them cut.

When Charlie landed, Seth greeted him with "How about a beer?" Charlie declined; then they climbed onto the swamp buggy. Seth cranked the engine, put it in gear, pushed the accelerator to the floor, and released the clutch. At first the odd vehicle remained motionless, its huge rear tires spinning wildly in the soft earth, and then it leaped three feet off the ground and crashed through a clump of bushes.

Charlie grabbed an overhead guard rail and hung on as Seth drove them southeast into the swamp, the accelerator still halfway to the floorboard. Mud was flying everywhere, and Seth crashed the vehicle into bushes and head on into the smaller pond cypress, sending up thick sprays of bark and bits of boughs.

Ponds were not skirted but simply crossed as they came, the wheels creating two streaks of bubbling muddy water right through the lily pads. Once Charlie looked back and shouted, "I think you hit the alligator!"

"Don't worry 'bout it," Seth shot back. "He can't hurt this contraption."

They slammed, bucked, and skidded for five miles, then Seth suddenly pushed in the clutch and jammed on the brakes. The buggy spun around and around and then came to a stop when its rear end rammed into a tree. Charlie left his seat abruptly and landed ten feet away, flat on his back.

For a moment Charlie was afraid to move. The wind was knocked from him, and he was sure that something must be broken. He could hear Seth say loudly, "Haw, haw, I gotcha that time, didn't I!"

Getting slowly to his feet, Charlie discovered that he was intact although his rear was caked with mud.

He looked at Seth and said, "I think my butt is broke. Do you always drive the buggy that way?"

"Naw," Seth chuckled, "I usually try to make some time, but I didn't want to go too fast with you along."

"You travel like the alligator," Charlie said, trying to brush the mud from himself but only smearing it. "What you could go around you just smash over. I think it is best that I walk back."

"Ain't no need to do that. I'll let you drive if you want to."

"You know I cannot drive that thing."

"Well, then, 'pears that you ain't got no choice except to ride or to walk." He laughed again, then he said, "I'll take it easy going back. I were just foolin' around, payin' you back for dropping that snake in my lap."

They took saws from the buggy and went about the task of cutting the knees, which were clustered around a small stand of not more than a half dozen bald cypress. They found knees of all sizes and shapes, some shaped like human heads, some in the form of animals, one resembling a troupe of ballet dancers, and many that had grown into twisted, grotesque patterns. A total of about twenty-five were collected.

Seth drove back much slower and by a different route. He stopped the buggy when he noticed a fresh gash cut into the side of a tree. South from this there were more such cuts, and to the west, across a treeless area of marsh, there was a line of stakes with red cloth streamers nailed to their tops.

Charlie said, "Those cuts are the same as I have seen twice on the south end of Gopher Creek."

"Them's survey lines," Seth said. "Somebody has been running section lines out here. What the thunder fer, you reckon?"

"I do not know," Charlie said, "but I have found them twice. I have seen no men in the swamp doing this."

"Ain't no sense in it," Seth said, getting down from the buggy. "Suppose you and me just mess them things up a mite. I'll take an axe and cut another line on the trees off to the east, and you pull up them stakes and move them a couple of hundred yards to the north of where they are."

"Will this not bring trouble?" Charlie asked.

"Shoot, no. Ain't nobody going to see us. And besides, we'll just be having a little fun. Ain't no harm in it."

"I will move the stakes, then," Charlie said, "while you mark the trees."

A half hour later they returned to the buggy, their tasks completed. Before he cranked the engine Seth said, "Ever time you see them marks down in the south swamp, cut a new line like I done there. And I'll be on the lookout for new ones, too. Ain't nobody ought to be running them lines out here, but we can shore have some fun out of them.

As soon as they reached the camp, Seth went to the store and brought out two beers. This time Charlie accepted gratefully. He was much relieved when he

jumped safely from the buggy, and had already decided against making any further trips into the swamp
on this vehicle.

Seth took one of the knees from the buggy, turned
it over in his hands and said, "Best way to get the bark
off is to steam 'um first. I've got a big pot out back so
I'll do it here. After we get the bark off we'll polish 'um
down real good. Them things is getting scarce and
ought to bring a couple of bucks apiece. The tourist
folks sure like to buy them. You'd think they ain't
never seen a cypress tree, the way they carry on so
over a hunk of wood."

"I'll come back in the morning and help peel the
bark," Charlie said. "I'm going home now and wash in
the creek. My britches are filled with mud."

Charlie could hear a rumble of thunder far in the
south as he poled the dugout away from Seth's camp.
Dark thunderheads had also formed, and the moss
hanging from the oak limbs was blowing northward.
Birds along the creekbank scurried along faster than
usual, and the wind felt damp and cool.

Just after dark the rain came. It was only a gentle
shower and not the downpour they so badly needed,
but it cooled the swamp and washed the limestone
dust from the roofs of the chickees.

SEVEN

IT WAS TEN DAYS after Kenneth Riles talked to Albert Lykes about the Surf Development Corporation project before he drove south to tell Billy Joe Jumper that he would have to move from the land. He turned east at Copeland and then took the narrow winding road that ran from the Turner River Grade into the swamp. This was his first time in this area, and he was apprehensive about finding his way. He was also worried about how Billy Joe would react when told that he would have to abandon his home. Facing an angry Seminole was not within his realm of experience. At first he thought of asking someone from Surf to perform this task but decided it should not be done by a total stranger. That could well make matters worse.

When he arrived at the wooden frame house he found, almost to his relief, that Billy Joe was not at home. His unpleasant task had been put off for a while longer. He drove on to Seth Thompson's fishing camp.

A few days earlier Riles had looked up land deeds for this area and had discovered the ten acres owned by Seth Thompson. The little plot was an island right in the center of the Surf property, and Riles knew that its value would skyrocket when the new development got underway. He had decided it would be well worth his time to try to purchase the property and later sell it to Surf. In time it would bring thousands of dollars per acre.

Soon after he had moved to the swamp, Seth's father had thought of buying more land and putting in an orange grove. As a windbreak he had planted a mile-long line of Australian pines on each side of the path leading to the house. The orange grove idea had been abandoned, but the pines thrived, their trunks shooting upward and their limbs growing into each other to form a thick canopy over the road. An eighty-year accumulation of fallen needles lay three inches deep on the ground.

Riles entered this tree tunnel and felt as if he had driven his car onto a deep pile carpet. He also felt as if he had moved back several decades in time. The sun was completely blocked out and the only sound was a soft moaning as the wind swept through the trees.

He drove very slowly as he neared the end of the road; then he parked the car in front of the little store and got out. For a moment he studied the house and the surrounding area; then he noticed the old fat man coming toward him from down at the creek.

Seth said, "Howdy, mister. Something I can do for you?"

"Are you Mr. Thompson?" Riles asked, thinking that from Seth's appearance, this old man would be an easy person to deal with, especially if he offered a fair price.

"That's right. I'm Seth Thompson. What can I do for you?"

"Well, Mr. Thompson, I'm Kenneth Riles, owner of Riles Real Estate Agency. Have you thought of selling this land?"

"Nope. I ain't never thought nothin' about it."

"I'm kinda interested in picking up some property in this area. Would you be interested in an offer?"

"As I said, I ain't never thought nothin' about it."

"What would you say to an offer of two hundred dollars per acre cash?"

"I'd say I ain't interested."

"Mr. Thompson, this is nothing but swampland. What do you think is a fair price?"

"To be honest, fellow, I just ain't interested at all. Now is there something I can do for you? I got some boats to work on."

Riles shuffled his feet and clasped his hands behind his back. "Mr. Thompson, I'll make one more offer. I'll give you a thousand dollars per acre cash. That's ten thousand for this piece of swamp. That's a real fine price, isn't it?"

"I done told you I ain't interested at all," Seth said finally. "Me and my pappy before me has been on this land since 1890. That's eighty-two years. And I intend to stay here a few more and be buried right over yonder under that big oak tree. Now excuse me. I got work to do."

Riles became angry. He had not intended to say anything about the Surf project, but emotion overruled this intent. "Mr. Thompson, you're soon going to have to sell this property or live right in the middle of a housing project! Maybe smack in the center of a golf course!"

It took several moments for what Riles had said to even vaguely register, then Seth asked, "What are you talkin' about?"

"Surf Development Corporation has purchased ten thousand acres of this swamp and is turning it into a housing development. You've got one little speck right in the middle of it."

"That's not true," Seth said, his fat jaw sagging.

"Yes, it is true. Some of the work will begin within a week."

"Well, it don't matter none," Seth said in a guarded tone. "As long as the creek is here I can make a living. It don't matter none about them houses."

"Mr. Thompson, don't you understand?" Riles asked, his tone now condescending. "There's not going to be any more creek. Drainage canals will be put in, and this entire area of the swamp will be drained and cleared of everything. There won't be any more creek and there won't be any more swamp."

"Does this include where Charlie Jumper and Billy Joe lives too?" Seth asked.

"Yes. They will have to move. I came out here now to tell Billy Joe." Riles assumed a look of deep sympathy and said, "Mr. Thompson, I understand how you must feel. You've lived here a long time, and you're fond of this place. But ten thousand dollars is a lot of

money. You could move into town and get a job somewhere."

"Fellow," Seth said slowly, his age now showing in
his eyes and face, "I ain't had on a pair of shoes in
more than twenty years. What kind of a job you think
anybody would give me?"

"Well, I don't know, Mr. Thompson, but that much
money ought to do you for quite some time. You want
to sell now?"

"No. No, I don't. I'd have to study on it some."

Riles took a card from his wallet and handed it to
Seth. "When you decide, here's where you can reach
me in Immokalee. And Mr. Thompson, I've offered you
a real good price. Remember now, you should give me
first chance when you make up your mind."

Seth watched as the car turned and entered the
stand of Australian pines and disappeared. For several moments he remained immobile, wondering if
what he had just heard was real or some sort of wild
dream. He went into the store and opened a beer.
When he came out, blinking in the sunlight, he looked
toward the weathered old house and noticed, as if for
the first time, that the front porch was sagging badly.

Billy Joe was swinging a machete, cutting bushes
along the canal that paralleled the highway, when the
car pulled onto the shoulder and stopped. He had re-
moved his shirt, and his brown chest and forearms
were glistening with sweat. Several other men were
working in a line on down the canal.

He immediately recognized Kenneth Riles and wondered why he had stopped. Riles got out of the car and came down to him. He said, "Hello, Billy Joe. I went out to your house to see you and your wife said you were working down here."

"Yessir, Mr. Riles," Billy Joe nodded.

Riles felt uneasy. He didn't want to let his emotions run away with him like he had with Seth Thompson. But this was different. This was only a matter of passing on information. The other was an attempted business deal.

"Billy Joe," he said slowly, "you remember me telling you that the land you've been renting has been sold?"

"Yes, Mr. Riles, I remember. I've thought about it a lot. Has the rent gone up?"

"No, it's not that." Riles paused for a moment; then he said, "The company that bought the land is going to develop the whole area into a housing complex. You can't stay there. You'll have to move."

"When is this going to happen?"

Riles was surprised by Billy Joe's calm reaction. He now spoke with more confidence, "Right away. Preliminary work will begin next week, and the land clearing part will be in full swing within a month."

"How much time do I have?"

"They're going to work around your place and give you as much time as possible. You'll have at least three or four weeks."

Billy Joe wiped sweat from his forehead. "Mr. Riles, what about my house?"

"Well, the company has authorized me to pay five hundred dollars to each person who is a renter and has improved the land."

"You mean five hundred dollars for my house, my sheds, my fences and everything? Mr. Riles, that place is all I've got for twenty-two years of work."

"I'm sorry, Billy Joe," Riles said, his eyes cast downward. "I'm just telling you what the company has authorized me to do. Maybe you could take the money and have the house moved to another location."

It was the inherited nature of Billy Joe's generation of Seminoles to take things stoically, but anger was beginning to germinate deep within him. He said harshly, "Where would I move the house to, Mr. Riles? Is somebody going to give me free land? And even if I could find some place, it would cost five times more than you have offered just to move the house and put in a new well. There's nowhere I could get that kind of money."

This change of mood startled Riles, and he suddenly felt extremely uncomfortable. Sweat stains were showing on his pale blue shirt. He said defensively, "Billy Joe, I sympathize with your situation, but as I said, I'm only following instructions. You know I would do better for you if I could, but I can't. All you have to do to receive the five hundred dollars is come by my office and sign a paper. I hope things work out well for you, and if I can be of assistance, just let me know." With that he walked quickly to his car.

As soon as the car pulled away, Billy Joe went to the foreman and asked permission to quit early. His sudden flash of anger had now turned to deep fear, and he was dumbfounded as to what he could do.

When he reached the Turner River Grade he stopped and got out of the truck. He sat on the bank and threw rocks into the river, thinking and wondering. His first inclination was to retreat further into the swamp, but he knew instantly that he must not do this for Timmy's sake. If he ran, like many of his people had run in the past, there would be no future life for Timmy. And he knew that he could not live along the Tamiami Trail. He had driven that highway many times, and he had seen many of his people reduced to the status of freaks in a circus, not by choice but by necessity to live. He closed his eyes and he could see the signs, Visit Joe Osceola's Indian Village, stop five miles ahead and See John Tiger Tail's Indian Village, the group of chickees behind the board fence, the souvenir shop in front, pay fifty cents and go through this door into the village, watch the Seminole wash his clothes, watch the Seminole cook, watch the Seminole eat, pay an extra quarter and watch the Seminole brave wrestle the alligator.

He knew also that he could not live in the labor camps to the north. He had once been to Pahokee, and he had seen the shacks one on top of another, stacked together like cordwood, the cheap whitewash gone and the roofs sagging, the bare dirt yards, the shacks so close together that they seemed to touch, crushing the life out of a man; and coming back, between Pahokee and Clewiston, he had seen the sugar cane fields stretch away to the horizon, mile after mile of muck so black that it looked like soot, and the land without trees or any place where a man could be alone; then the orange groves and the vegetable fields and more labor camps with their shacks jammed together row upon row.

There would also be no place for him on the reservation, where most of the land was either under water or so poor that it would grow only wiregrass and scrub cattle, and would not sustain even those who lived there now in scattered clusters of chickees and block houses.

The more he thought the more confused he became. This plot of land was all he had ever known. It did not produce much, but it was enough, and it was all that he needed or had ever wanted. It was here that his children had been born, and it was here that he had broken away from the old life of his father. Now his whole world must end and start anew in some strange and as yet undecided place.

He got back into the truck and drove along the narrow road leading into the swamp and to what had been his home, driving slowly, wondering what to say to Watsie and Lucy and Timmy, perplexed even more by what he could say to his father and mother.

When he came into the house Watsie was at the sewing machine, making the wedding shirt for Frank Willie. Lucy was in the kitchen, and Timmy was down at the pen, feeding the hogs. He took a can of Coca-Cola from the refrigerator and sat at the table. For a moment he sipped the cool drink in silence, and then he said to Lucy, "Have you and Frank decided on the date yet?"

Lucy turned from the stove. "No, Pappa, not yet." She noticed the grave expression on her father's face. "Is there something wrong?"

"Could you set the wedding for early next month?"

"Yes, Pappa. We are only waiting until the cattle branding is finished on the ranch where Frank works. He can speak to the preacher any time."

Billy Joe then turned to Watsie. "I have a thing to tell all of you, and I want no one to mention it to my father or mother. I will speak to them myself tomorrow."

Watsie stopped the sewing machine and came over to the table.

EIGHT

THE NEXT DAY Billy Joe drove alone to his father's chickees. He found Lillie at the sewing machine and Charlie down by the creek cleaning a turtle he had brought in from the swamp.

Charlie brought the meat to the chickee and put it into a pan. Then he sat at the table across from Billy Joe.

"I have something I must tell you, Pappa," Billy Joe said.

"We have something for you," Charlie said, his wrinkled face beaming. He reached to the shelf and took down a tin can, then he dumped the bills and coins onto the table. "We have sold many things, and we have over two hundred and sixty dollars to help pay for the television for Lucy and Frank Willie."

Billy Joe looked at the money, and then he looked up at his father. "Ah, Pappa, you and Mamma didn't have to do that. I could have managed it somehow."

"It is what we wanted to do," Charlie said, still grinning.

"Why don't you and Mamma keep this money. There are things you could do with it."

"It is our part of the gift," Charlie said, his voice firm. "It is what we want to do."

"All right, Pappa. It is appreciated. Thank you very much. Lucy will be proud that you and Mamma helped." Billy Joe was surprised by the money, but he wanted to shift the conversation back to his purpose in being there. He said, "Do you have coffee, Pappa?"

"Yes." Charlie poured two cups and came back to the table.

"I have something I must tell you now," Billy Joe said, sipping the steaming liquid. "You've always known that we don't own this land, haven't you, Pappa?"

"Yes, I have known."

"And you know that the land belongs to someone else?"

"The land belongs to those who love it."

"That is not exactly true, Pappa. The land belongs to those who have a legal paper in the courthouse. Pappa, this land we live on has been sold, and the new owners are going to clear the swamp and build houses here. We must leave this land no later than three or four weeks from now."

Charlie sat still for a moment, trying to digest what had been said. Lillie stopped the sewing machine and just stared at Billy Joe. Charlie finally said, "That is not true."

"It is true, Pappa. We must leave this land. Mr. Riles, the land man in Immokalee where I pay rent, has told me this."

"But we have been here all our lives. We know no other place."

"I know, Pappa," Billy Joe said, shaking his head. "But it is ended. I will get work somewhere, and you and Mamma will come and live with us."

Lillie was listening carefully to each word, but she remained silent.

"I will not leave the swamp!" Charlie said, defiance now coming into his voice.

"Pappa, there is no choice. The bulldozers will come soon and there will be nothing left here. You cannot stay, and you must accept that."

"I will speak of this no more."

"Pappa, don't make it any harder than it is," Billy Joe pleaded. "We'll discuss it some more later. There is time yet to decide what to do." He picked up the money and put it into his pocket. "This was a real fine thing for you to do. Now we can buy a television with the wooden cabinet. Lucy will be so proud of you. I will see you again tomorrow."

As soon as the truck was out of sight, Charlie went down to the creek and poled away in the dugout. He pushed the thin cypress pole in and out of the muck, moving swiftly. He still could not believe what Billy Joe had said, and his wrinkled face suddenly looked so old as to be beyond time itself, as ageless as the swamp.

Billy Joe had come to grips with reality and accepted what must be, and he had done this without bitterness; but he was of a different generation and a

different time than Charlie. The older Seminoles har-
bored a deep distrust for the white man, and even a
hatred. Charlie had heard his father and his grandfather speak of the time when the Seminole lived on
the land far to the north, the rich rolling hills with fer-
tile soil that grew corn and squash and pumpkin in
abundance, and the game was plentiful and the
streams as clear as an open sky, and then the white
man came and took the land, and there was fighting
and blood and death and hunger; then the Seminole
moved south, giving way to the white man, settling on
the land north of the big lake, but the white man came
again and wanted the land, more fighting and more running and more hunger, and they moved south again.
Then the white man said they could have this land and
be bothered no more; but he came again and the blood
ran red, and the white man brought in dogs to track
the Seminole like an animal. Then they placed a
bounty on the Seminole, fifty dollars for a man, twenty-five dollars for a woman, fifteen dollars for a child,
bands of white hunters surrounding the chickees at
night, capturing the men and women and children,
binding their hands and feet with rope, throwing them
into wagons like sacks of feed and hauling them to the
fort in the north where they collected the bounty and
returned to the swamp for another hunt; then the fighting and the running until the Seminole disappeared
into the heart of the swamp and into the Sea of Grass
and did not come out again until it was safe to do so,
and some had not come out yet.

Charlie himself had seen the white man come into

this land and slaughter the egret for its feathers, shooting them only when nesting on the rookery, killing them by the hundreds of thousands and leaving the young either to die in the nest and be eaten by vultures or fall out of the nest and drown, and the water around the mangroves turning red with blood; and he had seen the white man come into this land and slaughter the alligator, shipping out their hides fifty thousand at a time to be made into wallets and shoes, and he had once seen a thousand alligators killed in one pond in one day, but this time not for the hides, for the white men pulled out the alligator's teeth to be sold as watch fobs and left the bodies with their hides to rot in the blistering sun; and he had seen the white man come with his mules and his curses and his saws and his puffing trains and strip the land of the giant bald cypress, cutting them down like fields of sugar cane; and he had seen the white man wipe out the tree snails so that their shells could be sold as trinkets; and he had seen the white man dig the canals and drain the land and come closer and closer until he was now here again, once more telling the Seminole that he could not live on this land because the white man wanted it.

Before he realized it he had moved all the way through the swamp and come to the edge of the great marsh. He gazed for a long time across the swaying River of Grass, looking far to the south and even past where his eyes could see. The sun was beginning to set, and brilliant hues of red and orange and yellow were streaking through the clouds and downward into the hammocks, making the tops of the palms sparkle and glisten like tiny bits of rainbow. Even the somber sawgrass was changing color as the sun dropped lower into the west. There was a quietness about the marsh that made it seem not a part of this world, a land and a time completely unto itself. Darkness had almost descended when the old man turned and left, moving back into the swamp.

When he reached the chickees, Charlie ignored the turtle stew he always relished and sat by the fire. Lillie watched him but said nothing. It was late into the night when he finally lay down on the blanket and stared upward into the thatched roof. When Gumbo jumped up beside him, he put his arms around the furry little animal and held him tightly.

The next morning Charlie poled the dugout up Gopher Creek to Seth's camp. He found Seth out by the swamp buggy and walked up to him.

Seth said, "Howdy, Charlie. You O.K. this morning?" The usual smile was gone from his face.

"I am fine," Charlie said.

Both men squatted down and faced each other. Seth poked at the ground with a stick. "You heard about the land?" he asked solemnly.

"Yes, I have heard. Billy Joe told me."

"What you goin' to do?"

"I do not know, but I will not leave the swamp."

Seth suddenly jabbed the stick into the soft earth. He muttered, "Hell of a note, that's what it is. That's how come them survey lines has been run everwhere. They ain't got no right."

Charlie asked, "When are you going to Immokalee again?"

"I was planning on going this morning. You need me to bring you something?"

"No. I wish to go with you. I have a thing to do there."

"Well, you're plumb welcome," Seth said, struggling to get up. "We might as well go on right now and get back. I've got stuff to do here this afternoon."

Both men got into the battered pickup and Seth drove westward over the narrow limestone road. No further mention was made of the sale of the land, and the trip to Immokalee was made in silence.

When they reached the outskirts of the town, Charlie said, "Will you let me off at the office of the land man, Mr. Riles?"

"Shore," Seth grunted. "What you goin' to do there, buy up the swamp so's they won't run you off?" He said it without mirth.

"No, I just wish to talk. I will be waiting for you later in front of the building."

"I won't be long," Seth said. "I just got to pick up a few things at the hardware."

Charlie got out of the truck in front of the small concrete block building and went inside. The secretary glanced at his bare feet with distaste; then she asked, "Can I help you?"

"I wish to see Mr. Riles," Charlie replied.

"Just a moment and I'll see if he's busy."

The woman went into an adjoining room and returned momentarily. "Would you go in, please," she said, motioning toward the open door.

Kenneth Riles was sitting at his desk when Charlie entered. He looked up and said, "What can I do for you?"

Charlie stood in front of the desk and said, "I am Charlie Jumper, father of Billy Joe."

"Oh, yes," Riles said. "I'm glad to know you. Billy Joe is a fine man." He wondered immediately why this old man was in his office.

"I have come about the land," Charlie said. "Billy Joe has told me about the land and the houses, and he says that we can no longer live there. If you will forget this thing and leave the land alone, I will make it up to you."

Riles asked cautiously, "Just what do you mean, Mr. Jumper?"

"I will send fish and the animal hides and the jackets that Lillie makes and snake skins if you wish. Seth Thompson can bring them to you each week. I will do this as long as you want me to."

Riles scratched his forehead and said, "Mr. Jumper, I don't think you understand. I don't really have anything to do with that land except act as an agent. I'm not the owner and I have no say-so whatsoever in this."

"Will you speak to the owner?"

Riles was trying to think of a way to calmly end this ludicrous visit and conversation. He said, "Mr.

Jumper, the new owner of that land is not a man; it's a corporation. I can't speak to a corporation about fish and pelts and snake skins. They'd think I've lost my mind."

"I do not understand," Charlie said, puzzled. "Why would they not consider this offer? The things I speak of are worth money, and I will send more if they say I must. I would also make the little canoes. I will do whatever they say, and I could also send some cash each week."

Riles got up from the desk. He said slowly, "Mr. Jumper, I appreciate your coming by to see me, but there is absolutely nothing I can do. You should go on and make your plans to move."

"Will you not even speak to the owners about this?" Charlie asked, his voice subdued.

"There is absolutely nothing I can do, Mr. Jumper," Riles repeated. He put his hand on Charlie's shoulder and guided him through the door. "Good to have seen you, Mr. Jumper."

For a few minutes Charlie glanced up and down the street, watching the unfamiliar people and the rumbling cars and trucks. He felt uncomfortable, alien, and very foolish, and he wished that Seth would hurry on and take him back to the swamp.

NINE

IT WAS EARLY MORNING at the beginning of the
next week when Charlie heard the truck
amble along the limestone road, heading
east. He listened intensely and knew it was not Seth
Thompson, for he could recognize the sound of Seth's
pickup. He went to the storage chickee, took out his
bow and several arrows, and entered the woods between his camp and the road.

For several minutes he squatted behind a bush and
saw nothing; then he heard the rumble of another
truck as it approached. It was a pickup loaded with gasoline drums. He fitted an arrow into the bow and
waited.

Charlie fired the arrow just as the truck passed.
The thin wooden shaft struck the top of the cab, ca-
reened forward, and landed in the middle of the road.
The truck slowed for a moment, then it picked up
speed again and disappeared around a curve.

Another pickup followed fifty yards behind this
one. As it passed, Charlie fired an arrow that struck the
right door and bounced off. The truck screeched to a
halt, and a man jumped from the cab, came around the
side of the truck, and picked up the arrow. He ran
his hand over the slight dent in the door; then he

walked toward the bush where Charlie was hiding. For a moment Charlie did not know what to do. He had not expected the truck to stop. He was not sure just what he did expect, or what he hoped to accomplish with his attack, but the approaching man loomed suddenly as a menace that addled his mind. He put another arrow into the bow and pulled back on the string.

The man stopped and stared at the bush, then he turned and walked back to the truck, carrying the arrow with him. The bow string was still taut as the man got in the truck and drove away.

For several moments Charlie remained rigid, his eyes glinting with a strange and faraway look. He began to breathe heavily, and his hands trembled. He thought of how close he had come to firing the third arrow, firing at a form he had never before shot at in anger.

Very slowly he released the tension on the bow and dropped the remaining arrows. He turned and crept back through the thick woods toward the chickees, leaving the arrows on the ground where they had fallen from his sweating hands.

The pickup was parked to the side of his house when Billy Joe arrived home that afternoon. As soon as he stopped, a man jumped from the cab of the truck and came over to him. He held an arrow in his hand.

"You Billy Joe Jumper?" the man asked.

"Yes, I am Billy Joe."

"I'm Lawton, the foreman of the land-clearing

crew," the man said brusquely. "I got something to say
to you, and I ain't going to say it but once, so you listen real good."

"What is it?" Billy Joe asked, alarmed by the angry
tone of the man's voice.

"Your old man's been squattin' up there behind a
bush, shooting arrows at my trucks. Here's one of
them. We ain't got time out here to be playing no
damned cowboys and Indians with some loco old man.
You better put a stop to this silly crap right now or
we'll have that old man locked up. You hear?"

The words stunned Billy Joe. He said with diffi-
culty, "How do you know who it was who did this?
What makes you think it was my father?"

"Well, it was an old Indian squattin' behind a bush
right up there where that dirt trail leads down to them
chickees. I seen him myself, and started to go knock his
brains out but decided I'd let it go and speak to you
first. If it ain't your paw, who is it? Don't no other
Indians live up there, do they?"

"I can't believe he did this," Billy Joe said, his voice
subdued.

"Well, that ain't all," the foreman said. "Somebody
has been messing up the section lines we've surveyed,
and it wouldn't be hard to guess who. You better speak
to that old man right away. We don't want no trouble.
We're just doing a job, but if he pesters us anymore
we'll have to do something about it."

"I will speak to him now," Billy Joe said. "It will
not happen again, I promise you. Just leave this to me.
I am sorry."

"Well, ain't no real harm done yet," the man said in

a calmer tone. He turned toward his truck. "But for Christ sake, shooting at trucks with arrows! The old man must be getting daffy."

"I will speak to him now," Billy Joe said again, grateful that the matter would be dropped.

Billy Joe did not go into the house, and as soon as the man was gone he drove quickly up the road toward the chickees. The truck raced down the dirt trail and slammed to a stop, sending a cloud of dust into the cooking chickee where his mother and father sat.

He jumped from the cab, ran over to the table and shouted angrily, "Pappa, what is this thing you have done?"

Both Charlie and Lillie were startled by the loud and unexpected outburst. Charlie put down the bowl and said, "Why is it that you shout, son?"

"Pappa, did you fire arrows at the trucks passing on the road?"

For a moment Charlie didn't answer, surprised that Billy Joe knew of this, and then he said slowly, "Yes, I did this. But what is wrong in shooting the arrow in defense?"

"In defense of what, Pappa?" Billy Joe asked, becoming more exasperated.

"In defense of our land," Charlie answered calmly. "Our people have done this thing many times in the past."

"Oh, Pappa," Billy Joe said, sinking down to one of the stump chairs, "this is not our land, and it never will be. Can't you understand that, Pappa? For what you have done they could lock you in a jail cell or send you away to the crazy house."

"I have done no wrong," Charlie said, looking straight into Billy Joe's eyes.

Billy Joe shook his head. Then he said firmly, "Pappa, promise me you won't do this again. If you won't promise me this I will quit my job and move into the chickees and watch you every minute until we are gone from here. I do not want harm to come to you for such a foolish thing."

"I did not mean to harm those men," Charlie said softly. "I did only what I thought I must do. If I had meant them harm I would have used the rifle. I was only trying to frighten them away. It will not happen again, Billy Joe. I promise you. Do not quit your job because of me. I am sorry if I have disturbed you so."

Billy Joe got up and came around the table. He put his arm around Charlie's shoulder. "Pappa, please let it go," he said, holding the old man tightly. "Things are going to work out for us. You will see. I know how you feel, Pappa, but don't do this again. It can only bring trouble and sorrow."

"I will not shoot at them again, Billy Joe. I have given you my word."

Billy Joe walked to his truck. He turned and said, "I am sorry that I shouted, Pappa. I did not mean to do that."

"It is all right," Charlie said. "Every man has a time when he feels he must shout."

As soon as the pickup disappeared up the trail, Charlie pushed the food away and walked slowly to his dugout. Gumbo jumped into the slim craft, and the two of them moved away into the swamp.

TEN

For several days Seth had been alternating between surges of anger and periods of deep depression. He spent more and more time sitting on the bank of the creek, staring blankly into the swamp. He fried fish in the deep cast-iron pot over the open grill and ate it automatically, not really knowing or caring if he were eating fish or swamp cabbage or an alligator gar. Slim noticed this change but said nothing.

Many hours were also spent brooding about why this sudden thing must be. To Seth this camp deep in the swamp was a sanctuary, and here and only here could he feel comfortable and safe. He had lived this way of life for so long that change was beyond the realm of possibility. He had been free, totally free to do as he wished and dress as he wished and be alone when he wished. Solitude was no farther away than one of the boats in the creek or the swamp buggy parked by the side of the house. From this camp he could come and go into the outside world as he pleased, and elsewhere he would not have such a freedom of choice.

He was at first startled and then curious when he heard the loud clank of a bulldozer coming down the

steel ramp behind a flat-bed truck, and then he heard
the high-pitched drone of power saws. He stood motionless for a moment, his head cocked toward the
sound, listening. Then he ran into the house and
emerged with a shotgun. The pickup truck shot across
the clearing and bounded full speed into the tunnel
formed by the Australian pines.

When Seth reached the north end of the line of
trees, one tree had already been felled, and the bulldozer was starting to push it to one side. He slammed
on the brakes and brought the truck to a screeching
halt, its tires digging through the deep layers of needles and exposing a streak of bare earth. The shotgun
was in his hands when he jumped from the truck.

"What the devil you think you're doin' here?" he
shouted. One saw was biting into the base of another
tree.

The foreman got out of a pickup parked nearby and
came over to Seth. "What's the trouble?" he asked.

Seth waved the shotgun toward the men with the
saws. "How come they're cuttin' down my trees?"

"Are you Thompson, the fish camp man?" the foreman asked.

"Yeah, I'm Seth Thompson, and I want to know
why you're cuttin' down my trees. You ain't got no
right to do this. You're on private property."

"No, we ain't," the man said, eyeing the shotgun.
"The survey shows that your property starts a half mile
down the road. These trees are not on your property,
and we've been told to cut them. We're just doing

what we've been told to do, mister, and you better put away that shotgun."

The other workers stopped the saws and listened. Seth said, "I don't give a damn what a survey shows! My pappy planted them trees and you ain't goin' to cut them down. Now you better clear on out of here afore I turn this scatter gun loose on you."

"Old man, you're making a big mistake," the foreman said. "This won't do anything but get you in a heap of trouble."

"You're in a heap of trouble right now," Seth said, cocking the hammer of the shotgun. "You got just one minute to clear on out of here."

"All right," the foreman said, backing off. "We're not going to argue with that shotgun, but we'll be back. This is not your property, and we're just doing what we're paid to do."

The men got into the trucks and drove away, carrying the saws with them. The bulldozer was left to the side of the road. Seth turned the pickup and drove back into the tree tunnel and toward the camp.

It was noon when the green car with the red flasher on top pulled up in front of the little store and stopped. Con Drummond, the deputy sheriff from Immokalee, got out and came inside. Slim was standing behind the counter, swatting flies. "Where's Thompson?" the deputy asked roughly.

"He's up to the house," Slim said, revealing a row of snaggled, rotten front teeth that made him lisp slightly.

"Well, go and fetch him down here."

Slim left and in a few minutes Seth came from the house and down to the store. The deputy was standing outside by the patrol car. He was a man of thirty and wore a pearl-handled .38 Smith & Wesson revolver. He said, "Are you Seth Thompson?" He had never before been to the camp or known Seth.

"Yeah, I'm Thompson. What can I do for you?"

"Sheriff Tate sent me down here," the deputy said. "He couldn't come himself 'cause he's busy in Naples. Says he's a friend of yours."

"That's right," Seth said, pleased by the remark. "Me and Arthur Tate has been fishing together a heap of times."

"Well, what was all the ruckus out here this morning?"

"What ruckus?" Seth asked innocently.

"You know what I mean," the deputy said. "How come you been running around out here waving a shotgun?"

"Ah, that wasn't nothing much," Seth said, shuffling his bare feet. "I just run some men off that was cuttin' down my trees."

"Well, Thompson, those trees aren't on your property, and you've been put under a peace bond."

"What's that?" Seth asked, puzzled.

"It means if you cause any more trouble at all out here we'll have to arrest you and take you to jail."

Seth had a sinking feeling deep inside. "You mean I can't protect my property?" he asked.

"Hell, Thompson, that ain't your property," the deputy said harshly. "Can't you understand that? Those men could have had you arrested for pointing that shotgun, but they didn't. They just made out a peace bond. They really done you a favor, and you ought to be glad of it. Sheriff Tate told me to tell you to stay away from out there where them men are working and keep on your own property. Said he'd really hate to see you locked up, but he wouldn't have no choice."

"Well, I guess if that's what Arthur said, he ought to know," Seth said calmly. His voice then changed back to anger. "But you better tell them men to stay off my land! If they come on my land with them saws and that bulldozer they's going to be a heap of trouble!"

"They know where the line is, and you better be sure you do."

Seth sank down to the bench and said, "You tell Arthur hello for me. And tell him that the next time I come into Naples I'll bring him a mess of fresh catfish."

The deputy got into the patrol car. "Yeah, I'll tell him, Thompson," he replied. "And you stay out of trouble. I'd hate to have to come out here again."

An hour later Seth again heard the high-pitched drone of the saws. He got into one of the boats and disappeared up the creek.

ELEVEN

SINCE THE CONVERSATION with Billy Joe about the shooting of the arrows at the trucks, Charlie had acted on the outside as if any mention of the development of the land had never taken place. Each time Billy Joe came to the chickees to discuss the impending move, Charlie would listen and say nothing, only nodding his head as if to indicate that he understood. He was trying to shut the entire matter out of his mind, hoping if he did not think of it, it would somehow go away. But when he too heard the distant hum of the power saws and the crashing of trees to the ground he knew it was real and that it would not go away.

He did not venture down the road to see what was happening, and he did not want to see. So long as the banana trees and the oaks and the palms and the palmetto shielded his chickees from the sight of anyone traveling the gravel road, and so long as no intruders came down the path from the road, he was safe. He could hear the trucks as they rattled along a mere fifty yards from the chickees, but he would not dare go out again and be seen by anyone. He wanted it to appear that he and his little camp did not exist.

Billy Joe had been spending all of his spare time

away from the road job in building the chickee for the
wedding feast for Lucy and Frank Willie, which must
take place at the home of the father of the bride. The
chickee would be forty feet long and twenty feet wide,
and there were many pond cypress poles to be cut for
the framing and many palmetto fronds to be gathered
for the roof. There were also pits to be dug and spits to
be made for the roasting of meats.

Timmy had been the most depressed of all by the
news of the land development and the necessity to
move. He thought that this would separate him forever
from his grandfather, and he feared the unknown that
was to come. His father had kept him busy gathering
fronds for the chickee they were building, but on this
morning he had slipped away and come down to his
grandfather's camp.

One log had been left after Charlie had carved the
little dugouts which were sold to the souvenir stands,
and he was making this last canoe for Timmy. He was
driving chips from the center of the log when Timmy
trotted down the dirt path and dropped down beside
him on the ground.

Charlie looked up from his work and noticed that
the constant smile was missing from Timmy's face. He
said, "I am making this dugout for you."

"Really, Granpappa?" Timmy said without the expected enthusiasm. "When can I have it?"

"In a day or so. We will see how fast I can finish
it." He then put the log aside, looked at Timmy again
and said, "I think it is time you climbed the big
tree."

When he said this, Timmy became very excited. He asked quickly, "Can we leave now, Granpappa?"

"Yes, we will go now so there will be plenty of time. It is a long climb to the top of the sky."

Any thought Timmy had of ever leaving the swamp vanished completely as they drifted along this stream he loved so much. It was now only he and his grandfather and the trees and the vines and the birds and the turtles, and it would be so forever. No other thing existed as they moved deeper into the swamp, no trucks passing his house and no saws humming and no bulldozers moving about like huge angry tortoises. It seemed all too soon to him before they had crossed the ponds and the sloughs and were at the tree.

He asked his grandfather, "Can I see Forever Island? Which way do I look, Granpappa?"

"It is far away and to the south, but look hard enough and you may find it."

Charlie poled the dugout as far as he could into the thick knees, then Timmy got out and waded through the dark water to the base of the tree. He looked upward and it seemed to him that the tree had no end.

"Climb slowly and with a firm grip," Charlie cautioned. "Do not look down until you reach the top."

Timmy climbed the slanted base and reached the first rung, then one by one he moved upward, gripping one rung and stepping up, gripping another and moving upward again, feeling the wind grow stronger and stronger as he moved steadily upward toward the open sky. He was aware when he passed the roof of the swamp and there were no longer trees to the right and

left of his climb, but he dared not look down. He felt his arms and legs tremble as he touched the last rung and knew he had reached the top.

The part of the trunk where the top branches forked out formed a small flat platform, and Timmy stepped onto this and steadied himself against a limb. It was only then that he really opened his eyes, and he suddenly felt as if he had left the earth and joined a flight of egrets high above the swamp. He was fifty feet above the tops of the other trees, and the roof of the swamp looked like a long flat meadow punctured by stalks of dandelions which were the royal palms. He imagined that he could spread his arms and sail outward and upward, swooping and dipping and circling like a hawk. He looked to the south, and the River of Grass was a velvety brown mass moving endlessly, spotted with the green clumps of the hammocks, and when the wind blew, the strands of sawgrass swayed and weaved and tumbled. It seemed to Timmy that this was the world of the Great Spirit or God, and it would endure. Then he moved his eyes further south to seek the island, but the horizon was hidden from view. A solid wall of smoke drifted upward from the land and into the clouds, forming a link between earth and sky.

Timmy would have chosen to stay forever on this platform above the swamp had he not finally heard his grandfather calling from below. When he reached the base of the tree and stepped into the cool water he had to grasp a cypress knee and steady himself from the dizziness before he could cross to the dugout.

The trip back into the swamp was an anticlimax, and Timmy thought that surely he had just returned from a place where no one else had ever before been, and that he had seen things no one else had ever seen or would ever see. He lay in the bottom of the dugout and closed his eyes, and the things he had witnessed came back just as vividly as he had seen them from the top of the tree. It was a moment before he realized the canoe had stopped.

He sat up and watched as his grandfather chased crawfish up and down a shallow slough. Charlie was putting them into a tin bucket he had brought along. When he had all that he wanted he came back to the dugout and stuffed tree moss into the bucket to cover the flouncing captives. "I have enough this time for us and Gumbo too," he said. "Your grandmother will make us a feast when we return."

As Charlie got back into the dugout, Timmy suddenly reached out and struck at a swarm of dragon flies. His grandfather said, "Do not kill the creatures unless you have need of them. When you kill them without need you destroy a part of yourself."

"They're nothing but pesky old dragon flies," Timmy said.

"They are eating the mosquito," Charlie said to him. "Then the bird will eat the dragon fly, and the bird will help spread the seeds of the plants and trees. The deer will eat the plants, and then we will eat the deer. We all have need of each other, and I have told you this before."

"I didn't know that anything would eat an old mos-

quito for its meal," Timmy said. "I thought they were
only to bite us."

"The minnow will eat the mosquito also," Charlie
said. "The bass and the turtle will eat the minnow, and
we will eat both of them. The snake will also eat the
fish, and the alligator will eat the snake. Many years
ago we used the hide of the alligator to make our war
shields, and we ate the flesh of its tail. All things in the
swamp are important, Timmy, and you should not kill
without need."

"Then why are the men with the machines killing
the swamp?" Timmy asked.

For a moment Charlie didn't answer; then he said,
"Billy Joe says that it is because they will build
houses."

"Nothing can eat a house," Timmy said, not satisfied with the answer.

Charlie could not explain to Timmy a thing that he
did not understand himself, so he pushed the dugout
away from the slough and continued toward the creek.

When they reached the landing Charlie carried the
bucket up to Lillie and then took some of the crawfish
to Gumbo. He dropped them on the ground and
Gumbo grabbed them one at a time, scurrying in and
out of the storage chickee to eat them out of sight. He
bounded back and forth to the hut until there were no
more, then he climbed onto Charlie's shoulder and
scratched at his head. "Stop that, Gumbo," Charlie
said, putting the 'coon back on the ground. "Go down
to the creek and catch a fish if you are still hungry.
You have not forgotten how to hunt for yourself." As if

he understood, Gumbo rambled off down to the water's edge and paced up and down the bank.

Lillie chopped okra, tomatoes, peppers, and bay leaves into the pot with the crawfish, and put the pot over the fire to simmer. She would also fry halves of bananas over which they would pour wild honey. Charlie and Timmy sat at the table and waited patiently as Lillie whipped the corn meal into a batter to make the hot pone.

Timmy was still reeling from his climb into the tree, but he was disappointed by the smoke wall that blocked his view to the south. He said, "Tell me about Forever Island, Granpappa." He had heard the story once before but he could listen to it again and again.

"Not now, Timmy," Charlie said. "It is a long tale, and we will speak of it some other time."

"Have you seen the island?" Timmy asked.

"I am not sure," Charlie answered. "I could have been born there, but I am not sure of this. I have heard my father tell of the island many times. He knew it well."

"Will you take me there someday, Granpappa?"

"It is possible. Maybe we will go there together someday."

Timmy looked anxious for a moment; then he said, "Will the men take the machines to the island, Granpappa?"

"No, they will not do this," Charlie said. "The island is too far in the marsh for the machines to reach. They will never take the machines to the island."

By then the crawfish bisque was almost done, and

the aroma was drifting over to man and boy. Timmy got up and stuck his head close to the pot, sniffing deeply. "Is it ready now, Granmamma?" he asked.

"It is done enough for you," she said, stopping the sewing machine. "Sit at the table and I will bring it to you."

The distant hum of the power saws went unnoticed as Lillie crossed from the platform to the grill.

TWELVE

BILLY JOE DROVE DOWN the dirt trail and parked the pickup beside the cooking chickee. Lillie was at the sewing machine, and Charlie was sitting at the table sharpening the hunting knife he had used to carve the cypress canoes.

Billy Joe got out and took a seat opposite Charlie. He said, "Frank Willie and Lucy have set their wedding date, Pappa. They will be married a week from this coming Sunday in the Baptist Church on the reservation."

"They should be married at the Green Corn Dance festival," Charlie said, putting the knife aside.

"There won't be a festival this year, Pappa. Times are too hard with the drought, and the people have too much to do. Frank and Lucy want to have their wedding in the church."

"There should always be a Green Corn Dance festival," Charlie said emphatically. "It is a time to be together and sip the Black Drink."

"Pappa, you can get just as much good out of a dose of castor oil. The old customs are fading away. They're just not important anymore, especially to the young people." He got up, poured himself a mug of coffee, and returned to the table. "The wedding feast will be held at my place a week from this Wednesday. We have almost finished the chickee, and we have invited many people from the reservation and a few from the Tamiami Trail and the hammocks."

"I will kill the deer," Charlie said.

"No, Pappa, you don't need to do anything. The men from the reservation are bringing beef and turkeys and I will kill two hogs, and there will be vegetables and fruits enough."

"You cannot have a Seminole feast without venison," Charlie said. "I will kill the deer."

"Pappa, if you think you've got to do something for the feast, gather up a few turtles. Everyone knows that Mamma makes the best turtle stew in the Big Cypress."

"Do you think I am too old to hunt the buck?" Charlie asked, his eyes flashing.

"I didn't mean that, Pappa," Billy Joe said quickly. "Of course I don't think you are too old to hunt."

"I am the grandfather of the bride, and I will kill the deer," Charlie said with finality.

Billy Joe realized he was bucking a stone wall, so he dropped the subject. He turned to Lillie and said, "Mamma, do you need anything from the store?"

"I will need some cloth later this week, but I do not need anything today. Could you bring me a bag of the peppermint sticks? I have the money here."

"Forget the money, Mamma. I will bring them to you late this afternoon."

Charlie got up, went to the storage chickee, and returned with the little canoe. "Give this to Timmy," he said, smiling. "He knows I was making it for him."

"Thanks, Pappa. He'll be real proud. This afternoon he is gathering the last of the fronds for the chickee. I must go now. I will come back late this afternoon."

A few minutes after Billy Joe had left, Seth drove down the path and parked. As Charlie was still at the table, Seth took a seat opposite him.

"Would you like stew and corn bread?" Charlie asked.

"Don't mind if I do," Seth replied, sniffing the aroma coming from the grill.

Charlie dipped a bowl and handed it to Seth along with a huge piece of the hot pone.

Seth handed a brown paper bag to Charlie and said, "I been to Immokalee this morning and I brung you a sack of them sugar buns you like."

Charlie opened the package and took out one of the cinnamon rolls. "It is good," he said, eating half a roll in one bite. "I thank you."

"Well, it ain't near as good as Lillie's cookin'," Seth said. "You got the best dern cook in Collier County. She could stew a wildcat and make it taste good."

Lillie heard the remark and smiled.

Charlie said, "You want to gig frogs tonight? This time we could eat them ourselves."

"I can't make it tonight, Charlie. I got some business to take care of. We'll do it some other time, though."

"We will go whenever you wish," Charlie said. "The moon will be better later this week."

Seth finished the stew and got up. "Well, I got to go now. That was mighty good, Miz Lillie. I sure thank you."

"You are always welcome at our table," Lillie said, still pleased by the compliments.

As Seth walked to the pickup he turned and said, "You want to come with us tonight, Charlie? Me and Slim is goin' after a varmint that has been botherin' us some. We won't be out too late, and you're welcome to come along if you want to. You might enjoy it."

"Yes, I will go," Charlie said. "Will I need to bring my spear or the bow and arrows?"

"Naw, you don't need to bring nothin'. We got plenty to get this critter. I'll pick you up just after dark."

"That will not be necessary," Charlie said. "I will come to your camp in the dugout."

When Seth reached the camp he parked the pickup by the side of the house. Slim came from the store, and Seth handed him a package. He said, "Put this in the store, Slim, and you be real careful. It's dynamite. Them fellows ain't the only ones who knows how to use this stuff."

The moon would not come up until late that night, and it was pitch dark as Seth, Slim, and Charlie climbed onto the swamp buggy. Seth cranked the engine and turned on the lights. Then he headed down the road where the Australian pines had stood a few days before. The buggy stopped when they reached the place where the first tree had been cut.

Seth said, "You sure you brung it all, Slim?"

"I got everything you tole me to," Slim answered, "but I shore don't like ridin' on this buggy with a lap full of dynamite and blastin' caps. You take it easy, now. I know how you like to drive this thing."

Charlie was totally confused. He had surmised they were going after a panther or a bear that had been invading Seth's camp, and he could not understand why they were bringing dynamite and no rifles.

Seth drove for a mile through a section of dwarf cypress, following a set of tracks that looked as if they had been made by a dozen bull alligators. He stopped again when the tracks led off into a marsh area.

"Wouldn't nothin' but a dern fool try to drive a bulldozer through a bog," Seth said. "But they ain't going to have to worry 'bout getting it out." He gunned the engine and the swamp buggy shot out into the marsh, the beams of its headlights bouncing through tall clumps of cattails.

"Take it easy, Seth!" Slim shouted, the box bouncing on his lap.

The bulldozer had traveled a hundred yards into the marsh before its left track slipped into a sink hole, causing it to tilt badly to one side. Seth pulled up to the huge yellow machine and aimed the buggy lights at its gas tank.

"Hand me that stuff, Slim," Seth said, excitement in his voice.

Charlie was by then so mystified as to the purpose

of the trip that he remained silent and watched with increasing perplexity.

Seth took the package from Slim and walked to the bulldozer, his feet sinking out of sight into the muck. He worked for a few minutes in the beam of the lights, and then he hurried back to the buggy. "That fuse is long enough for us to get slam to China," he said, panting.

He gunned the engine and let off on the clutch with the accelerator full down, spinning the buggy around and almost throwing Slim and Charlie out. The little vehicle bounded off into the dwarf cypress as if it had been stung by a drove of hornets.

Seth stopped when they reached the road again. He turned off the lights, and the moment the beams went out they were engulfed in total darkness. It was as if the entire swamp had turned into a sea of ink, and Seth could not see Slim or Charlie sitting beside him on the buggy.

They sat in silence for several minutes. Then Charlie said apprehensively, "What is this thing you are doing, Seth? I thought we were going after the panther or the bear."

"That dern thing out there is a heap worse than either one of them critters," Seth said, "but I guess I ought to have tole you what we was up to. I thought you'd enjoy it."

For several moments they waited in silence, and nothing happened. Slim said, "I knew it wouldn't work, Seth. You don't know how to use that stuff."

"I know how to use it, and it's got to work," Seth

said, his voice agitated. "Maybe it ain't had enough time yet. It was a powerful long fuse."

Several more seconds passed, and then Seth said, "Let's go back and take a look. The wind could have blowed that thing out."

Just as Seth reached for the ignition key a mushroom cloud of fire shot upward above the trees, and was followed by a tremendous boom that rushed out of the swamp. The night faded away, and the entire area was bathed with orange light. The sound seemed to come again and again and shake the buggy.

After the fire cloud had dissipated high in the air it was replaced by a steady glow. They could not see the bulldozer itself from where they were parked, and the orange dome a mile away in the swamp looked like the reflection of a giant campfire.

"That's the first bulldozer I've ever seen blow up 'cause of a faulty gas tank," Seth chuckled.

"It do look kind of purty out there at night, don't it," Slim said.

Charlie was so frightened by the whole thing that he could not speak. He wished that Seth would drive the buggy back to the camp quickly so he could get in the dugout and leave behind the sight of the flames.

The three of them watched for a few minutes more; then Seth cranked the buggy and headed back to the camp.

Charlie wasted no time in leaving when Seth finally parked the swamp buggy beside the house, and the trip down Gopher Creek seemed to take only minutes. Lillie did not move when he lay down beside her in the sleeping chickee, and for a long while he stared upward into the fronds, thinking of what he had seen, wondering if his being present when this thing happened was a violation of his pledge to Billie Joe. This was what worried him the most, the possibility that he had broken his word to Billy Joe. But he did not believe he had dishonored his promise against further violence since he was completely unaware of the purpose of Seth's trip, and he had only watched.

It was late in the night when sleep finally began to come, and Charlie was only partially aware when he heard the flutter of wings coming out of the darkness of the swamp. He bolted upright when the owl lit on the roof of the chickee and hooted.

Lillie also stirred at the sound of it, and Charlie said to her, "Did you hear it? The owl lit on the roof of the chickee and cried out."

"Yes, I heard."

"It is the worst of all bad omens," Charlie said, deep fear in his voice.

"Maybe it is not so," Lillie said, also afraid but attempting to appear unconcerned. "Maybe it is just a tale."

"It is not just a tale," Charlie said emphatically. "The truth is written on the lives of our people. It is the worst of all bad omens."

She knew what he said was truth according to the customs of their people, but she did not want to increase his fear by showing her own. She said, "We must sleep now. Maybe the omen was not meant for us."

"This could be so," he said, "but it is bad for some-one."

It was hours later before either of them went to sleep.

It was mid-afternoon when the green patrol car with the red flasher on top came down the road and parked in front of the fish camp store. Seth was sitting on the bench, and he felt a tingle of fear as the vehicle approached. He was greatly relieved, however, when he saw that it was Arthur Tate. Somehow Tate repre-sented to Seth much less of a threat than the deputy, for he had fished with Tate many times but did not know the younger man.

The sheriff got out and took a seat beside Seth. "Good to see you, Seth," he said cheerfully. "Been a long time since I've been in these woods. Looks like there's a lot of stuff going on out here." Tate was a man in his mid-fifties, of medium height with gray-flecked hair and a yet trim waistline.

"Mighty lot going on," Seth said, his voice appre-hensive.

"Well, it's a shame the way they're chopping up the woods. Pretty soon there won't be any swamp left."

This remark put Seth's mind at ease, for it appeared to him that the sheriff was in agreement with his own feelings. "It shore is a shame, Arthur," Seth said ear-nestly. "Just a dern shame. They ain't got no right to be doing this."

Tate leaned back against the wall of the store. "How's fishing?" he asked.

"It ain't no good right now. Water's too low."

"I've sure made some good catches out here. Haven't had much time for fishing lately, though. Seems that folks just can't stay out of trouble, and they keep me busy all the time. I don't see why some people are so anxious to get inside a jail cell. I know I wouldn't enjoy it."

"I wouldn't enjoy it neither," Seth agreed, "but some folks just ain't got no sense."

"You ever use any dynamite around here, Seth?" the sheriff asked casually.

"I use some, but not a whole lot. Sometimes I blow out deep holes to trap the water when it gets down real low, like an ole 'gator will wallow out a hole to trap hisself some water, and sometimes I get rid of stumps to make trails for my buggy, but I don't use a whole lot of it."

"Looks like somebody planted about a dozen sticks on that bulldozer that blew up out here last night."

Seth said unsteadily, "Is that right, Arthur? That explosion mighty near throwed me out of the bed. I couldn't figure out what in the world done it till I went up there this morning and looked."

Tate looked directly at Seth and said, "Deputy Drummond tells me he checked around and found out that you bought some dynamite yesterday at the hardware store in Immokalee. You used it yet?"

Sweat was beginning to pour off Seth's face. "I shore have, Arthur. I blowed out a hole yesterday afternoon down close to an otter pond south of here."

"Well, I can't understand why anybody would want

to blow up a bulldozer, except maybe for pure mean-ness," Tate said. "It sure wouldn't stop this work out here because those big development companies have got a hundred other machines just like that one, and nobody could blow them all up."

"Don't seem like there's much point to it, does it?"

"Nope. No point at all. But somebody's going to get himself either killed or put in jail if he tries that stunt again. The company is putting guards out here at night, and I'm going to have a patrol in this area for a few days too."

"A man must be mighty crazy to do a thing like that," Seth said, trying hard to sound convincing.

"He sure is, Seth." Tate looked directly into Seth's eyes again. "We know that whoever planted that dy-namite used a swamp buggy to go out there, and we know he wasn't wearing shoes, because he left his prints all over the place, but that's not enough yet to make an arrest and go into court. There's buggy tracks all over the swamp, and half the Indians around here don't wear shoes. But we're still looking, and we'll be waiting for him the next time he tries it."

Seth glanced down at his bare feet, then over to the mud-covered swamp buggy parked by the house. He said slowly, "Man'd be a fool to try something like that again, wouldn't he, Arthur?"

"He sure would, Seth," the sheriff said. "It's just not worth it."

"If I see anything going on I'll let you know. I'll keep on the lookout."

"You do that, Seth. And you take good care of yourself. You've always been my friend, and I want it to stay that way. We've got to go fishing together again one of these days. There's not many good guides like you left."

"Anytime you want to go fishing, Arthur, you just let me know."

As soon as the patrol car was gone, Seth drove the swamp buggy down to the fish-cleaning stand and tried to wash the mud from it.

The pickup stopped at a small shack that had been placed beside the road and served as an office for the crew working this section of the swamp. A man got out of the truck and went inside. Two other men were in the shack, one sitting behind a small desk and the other standing.

The truck driver said, "Mr. Lawton, we're having some trouble around that marsh flat on the north end of the creek where we're trying to get that dragline in."

"How's that?"

"Well, the men have threatened not to go in there again. That whole place is swarming with cotton-mouths and rattlesnakes, and there's 'gators in there and ticks and chiggers and all kinds of varmints."

"You mean they're afraid of a few snakes?"

"They're not exactly afraid, Mr. Lawton, but have you ever seen a man after he's been hit by a cotton-mouth or a rattler? It ain't no pretty sight. And that place is a hotbed of them snakes."

"Well, take the pickup and drive up to Immokalee and hire one of those crop dusters. Tell him to come down here and drop some dieldrin and some DDT and anything else he's got to throw in the pot. We'll mark the right area with red flags. And while you're up there, get some arsenic and some meat and bait that place real good. We'll work around that marsh for a day or so, and by then all the snakes should be cleared out."

"O.K., Mr. Lawton. I'll go on up there right away. The men sure don't want to work in a hotbed of rattlers and cottonmouths. That place must be a regular breeding ground."

As the truck pulled away, the man behind the desk said, "Christ! First it's Indians shooting arrows, then it's a bulldozer blowing up, and now it's snakes. Next thing you know the men will be demanding hot lunches. But for Christ sake, snakes!"

THIRTEEN

CHARLIE HAD NOT HUNTED the deer in more than ten years, and the preparations for once again stalking this cunning prey were occupying all of his time. He had spent hours sharpening and sharpening again the tips of the arrows, and he had tested the strength of the bow at least a dozen times. In his lifetime he had killed hundreds of deer, and it had been a commonplace thing without excitement simply to obtain food, but this hunt would be different. It would provide the venison for the wedding feast of his granddaughter.

In his younger days the preparations for hunting the deer had consisted of simply picking up the bow and arrows and walking into the woods. Now he had spent two days doing the things that would have taken him five minutes in past times. Lillie watched him with amusement, comparing his anticipation with that of Timmy each time he set off into the swamp with his grandfather.

Billy Joe had said no more to him about the hunt, for he thought that Charlie would spend a few hours in the woods, fail, and then be satisfied that he had at least tried. There would be plenty of beef and pork and turkeys without the venison.

Charlie knew of a rye grass meadow on the south edge of Copeland Prairie where the deer grazed during the early summer months, and he would go there that afternoon to see if there were signs. He skirted around the area where the men were working and entered the woods to the north of the burned-out bulldozer.

The ground here was higher than the south swamp, and there were thick growths of buck vines and thorn bushes. As he moved further north the woods thinned out and there were more pines, and he knew he was near the edge of the prairie.

When he found the small clearing, he examined the wild rye grass and saw that the deer had been grazing there. Then he circled the meadow and found the trail the deer were using to go back into the swamp. The bark was skinned from several small trees where the buck antlers had struck them. Further down the trail he found a thick clump of palmetto that would be the best spot to lie in wait and ambush the buck as it came from its night feeding on the meadow.

On the way back to his camp, Charlie planned how he would kill the deer. He knew if he shot one at night while it was feeding and only wounded it, he would not be able to track it in the darkness. He would come before dawn and wait for the sunrise to signal the moving of the deer from the place of feeding to the sanctuary of the swamp.

That night after eating his supper and sitting by the fire, Charlie was too restless to sleep. He strapped on his hunting knife and started a journey that he could have waited hours longer to begin. With him he had the bow and three arrows, although in past days he had needed only one. Now his arms and eyes were not so sure.

The moon was high and full, bathing the swamp with a soft glow and silhouetting the dwarf cypress and the palms one against the other. A slight breeze, blowing from the north, rustled the fronds, creating rattling sounds. He was glad the moon was up and high, for he doubted if his old eyes could carry him safely through the swamp in total darkness.

When he neared the edge of the prairie he did not go to the meadow to see if the deer were there, for he feared he might startle them and run them away into the night. He walked slowly and softly to the palmetto clump and cleared a small circle on the ground; then he sat down and faced the empty trail.

As he waited for the dawn his mind drifted back through the years. There were times when he could hit the squirrel and the duck with the arrow, and he had once killed a black bear with only the knife. For a week before the Green Corn Dance festival the hunters would bring in game to be roasted over open fires, and there would follow five days of feasting and dancing and the purging of body and spirit. He could remember times when the deer were as plentiful as the birds, and he had watched them at play more often than he had hunted them for meat. As he thought of these things and tried to relive in his mind the vanished days of his youth, he gently and imperceptibly fell asleep, the ancient bow and the arrows clutched tightly in his hands.

Charlie awoke with a start and discovered the first red streaks of dawn tinting the eastern sky. The wind was still from the north, and that was good, for the deer would not smell him as they moved to the south. He had thought he heard a soft thumping on the trail, and he listened again and was sure. He inserted an arrow into the bow and waited. The sound moved again and stopped, then it moved forward and a small doe bounded down the trail and passed without seeing the man.

Two more does passed and Charlie waited, the arrow pointed toward the trail. He knew that the bucks always sent the does out ahead of them, and that the bucks would come soon. He waited for several minutes more; then he heard a tinkling sound which he knew to be the antlers of a buck striking vines along the trail. The deer moved forward slowly, its head cocked back as it sniffed the air. For a moment the deer hesitated, sensing danger nearby, and in that split second of caution, the arrow left the bow and struck the buck in its right shoulder.

The buck leaped high into the air and crashed into a clump of vines. Charlie scrambled to his feet and plunged after it, almost landing directly on top of the deer. For a moment the eyes of man and animal met, and before Charlie could plunge the knife in, the buck leaped to its feet and crashed off through the vines toward the swamp.

There was a pool of blood on the ground, and Charlie knew the buck was badly wounded. In other times his arrow would have stopped the deer instantly, but his arms were not now so strong. He would have to track the deer and keep it moving so that it could not stop to rest and gain strength.

The trail was not hard to follow, for there was a steady stream of blood along the ground and smeared on vines and trees. The buck moved south for a short distance. Then it turned east and veered along the edge of the prairie. He could hear the deer ahead of him, and several times he came to a pool of blood where it had stopped to rest, but, moving as fast as he could, he had not seen the buck again since he sent the arrow into it.

He followed the trail eastward for what seemed to be hours, and then the blood trail turned to the south. The line of the swamp between prairie and marsh was narrow here, and Charlie knew that if the buck continued straight south and reached the endless sea of sawgrass he would never find it.

The ground became much softer, and if it had not been for the drought he would not have been able to track through this area at all. The blood trail had almost stopped, but the tracks of the buck in the soft muck were easily visible.

When he finally stopped to rest, Charlie realized it was well past noon. He had no food or water, for he had followed the old custom of not carrying food on the hunt, and he had expected to be back at the chickees by now. He had known deer to run two or three miles after being wounded, but he must have already tracked this buck ten miles. It seemed that the deer

wanted to live as badly as the old man wanted it to die.

A mile from the marsh the trail turned and headed westward, and he moved steadily after the tracks. His throat ached but he dared not drink from the slimy ponds. He found a cocoa plum bush and picked some of the fruit. He did not like its insipid taste, but the kernel was mildly narcotic and would allay the hunger and thirst. After resting for a few minutes and chewing several of the kernels, he continued the pursuit.

Finally the trail came to the northeast end of Gopher Creek, and Charlie fell to his hands and knees, drinking deeply of the cool water. He bathed the cuts that covered his face and arms, cuts that he had not noticed until now. He could see the tracks continue on the opposite side of the creek, and for a moment he was not sure what he should do. The sun was now low in the sky, and if he turned for home, even without the deer, it would be dark before he reached the chickees. Perhaps Lillie would be worried and tell Billy Joe, and Billy Joe would come looking for him. He would not like this. He sat on the ground and cupped his head in his hands, trying to decide. If the deer ran much further it would be impossible to track at night, and he would lose it. But if he could not furnish the venison for the wedding feast of his granddaughter then he should sit on the platform and sew the jackets to be sold to the souvenir stands on the Tamiami Trail. And if he could not finish this hunt then he would not be strong enough to seek the island. He hesitated for a moment more, and then he plunged into the water and came out on the opposite side.

He followed the tracks but a short distance when he came to a spot of warm foam on the ground, and he knew that the buck was dying. Now he was glad he did not turn for home, for the hunt was almost ended. He began to trot instead of walk, and he found the deer lying in a clump of cattails. The buck tried to get to its feet but had no lifeblood left to do so. It struggled briefly and then fell back dead.

Charlie sank the knife into the deer's stomach and cleaned out the insides, then he pulled it by the antlers back to the creek and through the water. Once he could have put the buck on his shoulders and walked with it, but now he could not do so. He tried, but he could not lift it from the ground. He would have to drag it home by the antlers, and he hoped no one would see him doing this. It would not be in keeping with the dignity of a hunter.

It was two hours after dark when he reached the chickees, and he noticed the deep concern in Lillie's eyes. She handed him a steaming bowl of turtle stew, and he went to the table and ate ravenously. His arms and legs ached, but this did not matter. He would furnish the venison for the wedding feast of his granddaughter. After eating, he skinned the hide from the meat. From the hide Lillie would make a rug to go on the floor of the house trailer where Lucy and Frank Willie would live.

Later in the night, as he lay beside Lillie in the

chickee, Charlie's mind was completely divorced from all the things that had troubled him and given him anguish in recent days. As he hovered in that dream world between sleep and reality, he thought again of the old days and how it had been then when he brought the slain deer into his camp, how his children had gathered around him and stared in awe at the bounty that would soon become a family feast. The thought of the children reminded him of the days when he and Lillie had been lovers, of the nights when they had held each other close and listened to the gentle beat of rain on the thatched roof of the chickee, of the times they had wandered off into the swamp to be alone, and how they had once created life on a bed of thick green moss beneath the canopy of a giant oak.

Although his tired body ached for sleep, he thought of these things for a long while, then he took Lillie's hand in his and held it gently.

FOURTEEN

FINAL PREPARATIONS for the wedding feast were begun the day before the event was to be held. Billy Joe had taken leave from his job for two days, and he was up at dawn to finish the digging of the pits where the meats would be cooked. He had been both surprised and pleased when he went to the chickees and found that his father had made good his vow to furnish venison. He had taken the dressed deer back to his house. It would be roasted on a spit over an open fire.

Although Billy Joe and Timmy could have completed the necessary tasks alone, Charlie was present constantly, issuing instruction as each spade of dirt was turned for the pits and each frame erected for the roasting spits. Billy Joe was glad that his father was so totally occupied with the preparations and not thinking of what was to come in the near future. He pretended each task could not have been finished properly without Charlie's advice.

Jimmy Gopher arrived from the reservation at mid-morning with a dressed steer, and the wild turkeys would be cooked at the reservation and brought the next day. A pit three feet deep had been dug for the cooking of the beef, and a hickory fire in the pit was burning down to glowing coals. Billy Joe had cut thin gumbo limbo poles to put over the pit, and the beef sides would be placed on the poles and barbecued slowly for twenty-four hours. Shallow pits would be used for the cooking of the hogs and the deer, but this cooking would not begin until the next morning.

Lillie was making a pot of her turtle stew, for this was a favorite of everyone. There would also be a huge pot of boiled corn on the cob. This wedding feast was to be a substitute for the Green Corn Dance festival that would not be held, and there would be an abundance of all the favorite dishes associated with the festive event.

The traditional wedding shirt for Frank Willie was finished, and Watsie was busy in the kitchen making guava jelly to be served with the roasted meats. She would also make several pans of cornbread dressing laced with wild sage and the inner bark of the gumbo limbo tree. This would be baked and stuffed into the wild turkeys.

The huge chickee was also completed, and its size overshadowed the small wooden frame house. It would be used only once before the arrival of the bulldozers, but Billy Joe and Timmy had given no thought to this as they cut the cypress framing, gathered the fronds, and devoted so much time to its construction. A wedding was an important happening in the culture of the Seminole, and Billy Joe was determined not to let the impending move dampen the festivity of his daughter's marriage. As much as he could within his physical means, he would make this an event Lucy and Frank

Willie would always remember with pleasure and pride.

The activities continued throughout the day, Charlie trotting back and forth from one task to another, even invading Watsie's kitchen to sample the jelly and give it his stamp of approval. He tested the strength of the spits over and over again, and personally selected and cut the hickory limbs to be used in roasting the venison.

The next morning at dawn, Charlie and Billy Joe put the deer and the hogs over glowing fires and started them roasting, and soon the entire clearing became enveloped with blue smoke. The smell of the meats as they slowly browned was almost more than Timmy could bear.

The first to arrive at noon was Frank Willie and his family, then came Jimmy Gopher and Charlie Snow and Sam Huff and Richard Osceola and Josie Billie and Bird Fraser and John Tiger and Keith Whoyah and Billy Bowlegs and Miami Billie and Jimmy Cypress and Billie Tommie and Frank Jim and Jack Tiger Tail and John Poole and Ingraham Billie and Doctor John and Abraham Lincoln Jumper. There would be more than a hundred people present. All of the men were dressed in the traditional Seminole shirts that looked as if they had been cut from a rainbow, and the women wore the equally colorful ankle-length dresses. Even the young girls had abandoned their modern short skirts for this special occasion and were dressed the same as their mothers.

The guests arrived in bright red Mustangs and bat-

tered old Fords and Chevrolets and Dodges and pickups and two-ton cattle trucks with their high board
sides, some clean and shining and others coated a dull
gray with the limestone dust or caked with mud. Construction workers passing on the gravel road wondered
what was happening here in this remote section of the
swamp to bring together such an assemblage.

The older men at first wandered around the clearing, inspecting the fences and the sheds and the cattle
and hogs, staring dejectedly at the blistered vegetable
field, sucking grass stems as they moved from one area
of the property to another. Then they came back to the
house and huddled in a group, talking freely about
hunting and fishing and cattle prices and crops and the
drought. Some of the women busied themselves around
the cooking fires while others ran after the younger
children, scolding them for throwing rocks at the hogs
or chasing the chickens, threatening them with dire
things to come if they went into the swamp and ruined
their freshly starched clothes. The older boys and girls
began a game of stick ball, in spite of the heat. Charlie
partook of it all, leaving the cluster of men where he
enjoyed the esteem of the patriarch, going next to the
cooking fire where he cautioned the women not to
burn the venison, then shouting encouragement to the
stick ball players before returning to the gathering of
men.

Charlie had invited Seth to attend, and he arrived
two hours after noon. In the back of Seth's pickup
there were four washtubs of iced beer. From that point
on the men seemed to move steadily from the shade of

the chickee to the rear of Seth's truck and back into the shade again.

At four in the afternoon the meal began, and the eating continued for more than three hours. Knives were placed by each roast of meat so the guests could carve their own portions, and Charlie urged each person to take a larger cut. The only concession to modern times was the paper plates Billy Joe had purchased at the store in Copeland.

All of the men ate together in one section of the chickee, but the women separated themselves into small groups according to clans. It was against the old customs for women of different clans to eat together, and the little groups off to themselves represented the Panther, Wildcat, Tiger, Bird, Otter, Wolf, Snake, Wind, and Town Clans. This custom was seldom observed anymore, but all of the people were following the old ways as closely as possible for the last gathering here in this part of the swamp.

When the feasting was finally finished, everyone came together and sat on the ground beneath the chickee, the men in the front rows and the women and children behind them. Charlie wanted Billy Joe to present the wedding gift before the telling of the tales, and he and Timmy brought it from the feed shed where it had been hidden for the past several days. Lillie clapped her hands with joy as Billy Joe stripped away the cardboard box, revealing the new television set with the gleaming wooden cabinet. Lucy ran to her father and threw her arms around his neck.

"Don't thank me," Billy Joe said, embarrassed but

pleased by his daughter's open display of emotion. "This is mostly the doings of your grandfather and grandmother. It is their gift also, and you should thank them."

She ran to the old man and the old woman and kissed them on wrinkled cheeks. Charlie grinned broadly, and Lillie clapped her hands again.

The gift presented, it was now time for what they had all looked forward to, the telling of the tales. Everyone suddenly became attentive, and a silence fell over the chickee as they waited for someone to speak. Ingraham Billie then led off, saying, "I will tell of a man named Roosevelt Otter, and of the wildest ride in the Everglades. It was in the days when we caught the alligator alive and sold him to the tourist places in Miami and on the Trail. This Roosevelt Otter would come up to the alligator in his canoe, and he would leap on its back and wear it down until he could close its jaws and tie them. He was far to the south one day when he came to a giant 'gator. When he leaped on its back he found that it was not a 'gator, but a crocodile. He knew right away he had committed a grievous error. The crock's jaws were flailing like the blades of a windmill, and if he jumped off there would soon be no more of him than dinner in the belly of the crock. The only thing to do was ride it out as best he could. The crock was jumping and bucking like a stallion, but Roosevelt Otter hung on, his legs locked around the belly of the crock. They flattened several square miles of sawgrass, and two hammocks were destroyed completely. The ground for miles around looked as if the hurricane had come through."

Ingraham Billie stopped, and John Tiger, expecting more, asked, "Well, what became of Roosevelt Otter?"

"I do not know. The last anyone saw of him he was still on the crock's back, heading across Whitewater Bay and toward the Keys."

Seth spoke up and said, "Shoot, that fellow wasn't so tough. Once they was a catfisher up at Lake Okeechobee who could whup any ten men standing. Nobody never did know his name, but they called him Pogy, and he was something else. Didn't nobody mess with Pogy and come away with less than two broken arms or a busted head. Ole Pogy could pick up a two-hundred pound barrel of fish with his left hand.

"Well sir, back in them days Okeechobee City was about the wildest place this side of hell and back. Things went on there that folks nowdays just wouldn't believe. Ever Saturday all the cowpokes from north of the lake would come in, and all of the catfishers from down south would come in, and they had a standin' agreement to fight ever Saturday night soon as they got likkered up enough.

"Well sir, one Saturday night they'd all got skonked and gone to fist city about ten o'clock, and after they got done fighting, about a dozen of them catfishers decided they was hongry for some sweet stuff, so they goes to Albert's Bakery and bangs on the door till ole Albert comes out of the back of the store, where he lived. When Albert seed what was out there, he knowed he were in a heap of trouble if he didn't let them in and in a heap of trouble if he did, but he didn't want his door smashed, so he lets them in and starts dishin' up them pies and cakes. Soon as they got done eatin' somebody pulls out a pistol and starts shootin' up a shelf of canned peaches, and then the whole crew starts blastin' peach halves and syrup all over the place. I come by the store about then and seed what was goin' on, so I goes inside and takes advantage of the situation. Whilst all the ruckus is goin' on I eats me a half dozen of them blueberry pies. And all the while ole Albert is standin' in a corner, shakin' like a pine tree in a hurricane.

"When everbody leaves I follow them down to Gussy's joint where they all start drinkin' again. Well sir, ole Albert and Pogy is good friends, and when Pogy finds out what them catfishers done, he comes into Gussy's madder'n a bee-stung wildcat. He tells them fellows to dish up twenty dollars apiece to pay for the damages, and if they don't he'll make their heads look like a sack of hickernuts. And he woulda, too. One of them fellows says he ain't goin' to pay no twenty bucks just for some canned peaches, so Pogy picks him up and slams him clear through the wall, right out into a pen full of hogs. Then Pogy says it'll be another ten dollars apiece to pay for Gussy's wall. Them fellows seed right away the longer they waited the more it was goin' to cost them, so they all dished up the cash on a table.

"Pogy picked up that money and started out to give it to ole Albert, and one of them fellows spoke up and said, 'What about Seth? He et six pies and didn't pay nothin'.' With that Pogy looks at me and says, 'That'll be two bucks each for the pies, Seth.' I didn't have a cent on me, so I says, 'I ain't got no money, Pogy. I swear I'll pay Albert next Saturday soon as I get my fish pay.' Ole Pogy looks at me even harder and says, 'Seth, you mean you et six of Albert's pies and ain't got no money to pay?'

"Well sir, when I says 'yes,' ole Pogy moves closer and says, 'Seth, if you done et them pies and you ain't got the money to pay, best I can do is see to it that you don't enjoy them.' With that he hauls off and hits me in the stomach so hard his fist goes plumb through my gut and rattles my backbone. And you know, ole Pogy wasn't tellin' no lie 'bout me not enjoyin' them pies. As soon as that big fist comes out of my belly I double up and start pukin' everwhere. I throwed them pies up all over the floor and all over Pogy's shoes, and that done it. Pogy he makes me take off my shirt and clean that puke off his shoes, then he tells me I got to wear that shirt without washin' it until I pay Albert or he'd knock me slam down to Big Cypress. And I knowed he'd do it, too. So I wears that shirt for a week out in that broilin' sun. You ever smelt week-old blueberry puke? I swear to this day I ain't never et no more blueberry pie, and I ain't likely to, neither. But that Pogy was something else, fellows. Could whup any ten men standing."

Sam Huff then said, "That is a good tale, Seth Thompson, but this sickness you speak of is nothing. I have seen worse. Before we moved to the hammock we lived in chickees along the Tamiami Trail, and the tourist people were always stopping and tromping through our place, just like it was some kind of a public zoo. Early one morning this man stopped his car and came to the chickee and said he was some sort of a writer, and that he wanted to know about the Seminole. We didn't pay him any mind, but he kept following us around, writing in a notebook and playing one of those recording machines. Every time I made a move he was right behind me. I believe if I had pooted he would have run up and smelled it just so he could say that he had smelled Indian poot.

"He kept this up all morning, and at noon he said he would give me five dollars to let him squat down in the chickee and eat Seminole food like we eat. I told him I didn't run a cafe but if he was hungry we would give him food. Sara had a big pot of rabbit stew going, so she dished him up a bowl and he squatted down and started eating. He really made a big show of it, too. It wasn't anything but plain rabbit stew, but he kept groaning and grunting about how good it was and what a surprise it was to know that Seminoles ate such good food. Then he asked me what was in the stew so he could make it himself sometime.

"I looked real solemn and said, 'This is a favorite old Seminole dish. It is part skunk, part cottonmouth, part dog, and part buzzard. If you like it so much we will give you a jar to take with you.'

"That tourist man dropped the bowl, and for a few seconds I thought he was going to faint. He just swayed back and forth, his face as white as the egret's feather. Then he started to vomit. Seth Thompson, you think you did something with those pies; you did nothing. That fellow beat all I have ever seen. He finally ran down to the canal and stuck his whole head beneath the water, plumb down to his shoulders, and he just squatted there for five minutes with his head under the water. I thought he had drowned himself. Then he jumped up and ran for his car, and didn't say another word to anyone. He even left his notebook and the recording machine and didn't come back for them, either. We never saw him again, and I gave the recording machine to my cousin Tommie Toby. His wife uses it to store her needles and thread."

Josie Billie, the Baptist preacher on the reservation, spoke up and said, "I will tell a tale of religion."

Charlie interrupted, "I would rather hear a hunting tale instead."

The preacher looked at Charlie. "Are you not a religious man, Mr. Charlie?" he asked.

"I was once a Baptist, like you," Charlie answered. "It was long ago, and the white missionary came to me and told me that the Indian way was all wrong, that if I ever wanted to see the Great Spirit I would have to become the Baptist and do it the white man's way. So I became the Baptist. And then another white missionary came, and he was the Methodist. He told me that the Baptist way was not the right way, and if I wanted to see the Great Spirit I would have to become the Methodist. So I became the Methodist. And then yet another white missionary came, and he was the Presbyterian, and he told me that the Methodist way was not the right way, and if I wanted to see the Great

Spirit I would have to become the Presbyterian. I said to him that if the white men cannot decide among themselves which is the right way I will become the Indian again and seek the Great Spirit in my own way. And that is what I have done, Josie Billie, and I will see the Great Spirit when the time comes."

The preacher laughed, then he said, "Well, Mr. Charlie, if you ever decide you want to start all over again and be a Baptist, you will be welcome at our church on the reservation. I am no missionary, only a simple preacher, and I will not tell you that only one way is right."

Timmy jumped up and said, "Let Granpappa tell of Forever Island."

"I have heard of it," John Hicks said. "It is in the Ten Thousand Islands."

"No, it is not," Charlie said quickly. "It is in Pa-Hay-Okee. My father once lived there, and I have heard him speak of it many times."

"There is no such place," Billy Joe interrupted. "When our people had to hide from the white soldiers, all of the swamp and all of the Glades was Forever Island. It is everywhere, and there is no such one place. Forever Island is only a tale that has grown with time."

"You are wrong, Billy Joe," Keith Whoyah said. "I have also heard my father speak of it."

"Let Charlie tell it," Bird Fraser said. "I want to hear it from him."

"It was many years ago, in the days of my father and before," Charlie began, his eyes taking on a far-away look as if he were now in the top of the giant tree

himself, seeing over and beyond the roof of the world
and through the borders of time, seeking something far
in the past. "The third war with the white soldiers had
ended, and our people were living here in the edges of
the great cypress swamp. But the white men passed a
law that none of our people could remain, and an offer
of money was made for the capture of the Seminole
man, woman, and child. Our people were to be sent to
the lands in the west where others of our nation had
already been sent by the white soldiers.

"Our people would not leave, and they fled deeper
into the swamp. They had to eat snakes and roots and
whatever they could find, and they ate the fish raw for
fear that smoke from the cooking fire would give them
away to the white hunters. Then the white soldiers
came again, and the people moved south once more.
Some fled to the Ten Thousand Islands and hid there,
and some went many days travel into Pa-Hay-Okee,
and it was there in the River of Grass that they found
Forever Island. It was the largest of all hammocks, and
it had never been seen by the white man.

"The island was surrounded by a reef of limestone
rock, and a shallow moat ran from the rock to the
shore. The game was plentiful, and the fish as thick as
the blades of sawgrass. There were deer and rabbit and
squirrels and the turkey flew among the trees. In the
center of the island a deep spring brought forth great
quantities of cool water. From the rich soil they grew
corn and beans and pumpkin, and there was a large
grove of banana trees and also guava, mango, and pa-
paya.

"The trees were of many kinds, the oak and the strong mahogany and the gumbo limbo and the palm and the lancewood from which the fish spears were made. The muscadine was plentiful, and there were wild oranges on a hammock nearby. It was an island unlike all others.

"Our people lived there for many years. Then a great fire in the sawgrass came out of the south, near where the white man had built the village called Miami. It came toward the island with a great roar, and the people fled to the north, leaving behind all but their spears and their tools. From a distance they watched the flames leap into the trees and through the village, and then they could see no more. They went to other hammocks out of reach of the fire, and many came back to the swamp. That was many years ago, and now the island would show no scars from the great fire. It should be now as it was then."

"But how would you ever know this island today?" John Tiger asked. "Would it not look the same as many other hammocks?"

Charlie responded, "It is said that the people built a stone pyramid ten feet high in the middle of the island as the center of the Green Corn Dance. The fire would not have harmed the stone, and you would know the island by the pyramid."

"That is a good tale, Pappa," Billy Joe said, "but it is nothing more than a tale. You are right now in the center of Forever Island."

Two more tales were told, one of hunting and one of the great war. Then Charlie suddenly jumped to his feet and said, "Let us do the Green Corn Dance! It is not a proper wedding feast without the dance."

"Yes, let us do it!" Miami Billie echoed.

"But we will need the beat, and we have no drums," Sam Huff said.

"We can use tubs," Jimmy Cypress said, the enthusiasm spreading quickly.

"I will bring two tubs from the feed shed," Billy Joe said.

Several of the men gathered limbs and small logs and threw them onto the coals in the pit where the beef had been cooked, causing a stream of sparks to shoot upward into the darkness.

Billy Joe returned with the tin tubs and handed one to John Tiger and one to Josie Billie. The women and children moved from the chickee and sat on the ground, forming a huge circle around the growing fire.

As an irregular, staccato beat came from the tubs and echoed around the clearing, Charlie stepped inside the circle, standing rigidly erect for a moment, his arms reaching upward into the night sky as if trying to grasp the darkness. Then his feet began to move, slowly at first, like a child playing hopscotch, then faster and faster, his feet barely touching the ground.

One by one the men joined the dance, all of them now chanting as their arms flailed the air. The tempo of the dance increased as the flames shot higher, bathing the clearing with an orange glow and sending shadows through the trees and into the swamp. Faster and faster they danced until they were mesmerized, performing a ritual that had been repeated a hundred times before in other glades across this swamp but would not be repeated again. The dancers sensed that this night was the beginning and the end and they wanted to make the most of it.

Charlie danced wildly, as if testing his old body to the limits of its endurance. Then he fell exhausted to the outside of the circle. His eyes gleamed as he watched the other men continue until they too, one by one, dropped out and fell to the ground, panting and sweating. Just as suddenly as it had begun, the Green Corn Dance was then ended.

It was after midnight when the procession of bright red Mustangs and battered old Fords and Chevrolets and Dodges and pickups and limestone-coated cattle trucks left this remote spot in the swamp and started back toward the Turner River Grade and another world.

FIFTEEN

THE MORNING AFTER the wedding feast Seth walked down to the creek to take one of the boats and check a fish trap north of the camp. He suddenly started shouting, "Goddammit! Slim! You come down here, Slim!"

The lanky man scrambled from the store and ran down to the water, wondering what had brought on this unexpected outburst.

"Look at that, Slim!" Seth bellowed. "Look at that! They're ruining the creek!"

A gray streak of mud silt had come down the center of the creek and was widening out toward the banks.

"It's that damned dragline they got workin' up north of here," Seth said. "They'll run ever fish out of here for ten miles around."

Seth paced back and forth for a few minutes, then he said to Slim, "I'll go take up them lines and traps afore they get covered by the mud. You take the truck and go down to Copeland and get me two five-gallon cans of gas. We'll do it this time with something everybody uses; then they won't be able to trace nothin' to me. Goddammit!"

It was just after dark when Seth and Slim put the gasoline cans into the boat and started up the creek. Seth said, "A boat sure don't leave no tracks, do it, Slim?"

"It sure don't," Slim answered, as unconcerned as if they were starting out to set fish traps.

"And I'll fool 'um this time with these shoes."

Seth had put on a pair of brogans so old that the leather had decayed in several places. He had slipped them on without laces so they wouldn't hurt his feet. As soon as the job was finished and he was back in the boat, he would take them off and sink them in the creek.

They used a boat without an engine so as to make no noise, and Seth sat in the rear and paddled while Slim rode the elevated bow. It was two miles up the creek to where the dragline was stationed.

As they rounded a bend they could see the dragline silhouetted by the moonlight. Seth turned the boat into the bank and they got out, Slim bringing the two cans.

Seth said, "I'll slosh the stuff on this side and you slosh it on the other. Then you get back in the boat and I'll throw the match. That thing ought to go up like a bunch of dried sawgrass. Then we'll hightail it back down the creek and nobody'll know the difference."

Slim went around behind the dragline while Seth poured gasoline on one side. Seth was halfway through the can when a brilliant beam of light came from about fifty yards across the marsh and centered on him. He heard someone shout, "Hey! What you doing out there? Drop that can and come on over this way!"

For a moment Seth froze, thoroughly frightened and addled by the unexpected light and the shouting from the darkness. He turned toward the beam and was blinded, and then he dropped the can and jumped from the dragline.

He heard the shouting again, "Hey, fellow, you! Stop right there!"

Seth's eyes were blinded by the light, but he ran toward where he thought the boat should be. There was a thin flash of fire followed by a loud explosion. He felt something hit him hard in the left chest, and he went down to his knees. For a moment he stayed down. Then he struggled to his feet and stumbled into the creek.

The boat was not there, and he could hear no sound from Slim. Then he waded across the shallow water and disappeared into a thick clump of willows on the opposite side.

Seth's foot had struck the right side of the boat when he entered the water, and now the boat was floating slowly down the creek, empty.

Charlie was sitting at the table the next morning, eating a bowl of corn grits, when the green patrol car came down the lane and stopped. Sheriff Tate got out and came over to him.

"You been out in the swamp yet this morning, Mr. Jumper?" the sheriff asked.

"Yes, I have been there," Charlie answered, pushing the bowl aside. He had been to the pond to feed Little George.

"You see anything of Seth Thompson?"

"No, I have not seen him. Is something wrong?"

"Yes, I'm afraid so," the sheriff said, concern in his voice. "Seth was in a little trouble last night, and I think one of the company guards shot him. He may be needing help very badly."

"Is he in much trouble when you find him?" Charlie asked, dismayed by the news, thinking immediately of the night he had accompanied Seth and Slim when they destroyed the bulldozer.

"Not too much. He hadn't really done anything before this guard popped off his rifle at him. He's in some trouble, but not too much to handle, and he'll be O.K. if I can just talk some sense into him and get him to stop right now. But the important thing is to find him."

"I will help you do this," Charlie said eagerly, getting up from the table.

"We'd sure appreciate it, Mr. Jumper. I've got a swamp buggy up at Seth's camp, and we're going to look in those woods on the north side of the creek. You try anywhere you want, and we'll see you later at the camp."

Charlie got into the dugout and poled swiftly up the creek. The mud had not come down this far yet and the water was clear, but when he approached the camp the creek was a solid gray.

He continued past the camp and moved the dugout even faster. There was a small shack to the south of the creek where Seth sometimes stored fish traps when they were not in use, and Charlie thought that this was where Seth would probably be.

He pushed the dugout onto the bank and walked through an area of dwarf cypress; then he came into a cabbage palm hammock. The little shack was to the left, and he saw Seth sitting on the ground, leaning back against the trunk of a palm.

Charlie ran to him and dropped down to his knees. "Are you bad?" he asked.

"I ain't too good, Charlie," Seth answered, his voice weak, "but it sure is good to see you here." The shoes were gone, sucked off by the muck as Seth fled through the swamp, and his overalls were caked with mud. Blood from a hole in his chest had run down and mixed with the dried mud.

"I will take you back to the camp," Charlie said.

"Ain't no use to try that. I'd just sink that little ole canoe you got. You go to my place and get one of the boats and then come on back. And when you come, Charlie, bring me a can of cold beer. A man can't travel on one leg, you know."

Charlie got up and said, "I will be back quickly, Seth. You will be all right soon."

When Charlie reached the camp the sheriff and three other men were there. "You seen anything of him yet?" Sheriff Tate asked anxiously. "We didn't find a trace of him north of here."

"I have found him," Charlie said. "He is to the south of the creek, and he is hurt badly. We must get him out at once."

The company guard spoke up and säid, "There were two of them up there last night, sheriff."

"The other would have been Slim," Sheriff Tate said. "If you missed him with that damned rifle he's probably in Georgia by now."

"I told the fat one to stop," the guard said. "I hollered at him three times."

"You sure did want him to stop, didn't you," the sheriff said angrily. He then turned to one of his deputies. "We better take two boats up there. Seth is a big man, and only one person can ride with him coming back."

Charlie ran to the store and got the can of beer, and then he led them up the creek. When they reached the palm hammock Seth was still sitting on the ground, his eyes closed and his hands dropped down by his sides. Sheriff Tate leaned over him and said, "Well, he didn't make it. He's dead."

Sheriff Tate then put his hands over his eyes and said, "Poor old fellow. He did the only thing he knew to do. If I could have talked to him just once more I might have been able to stop this."

Charlie looked at the guard and said angrily, "You did not have to do this! You will be cursed for the rest of your days!"

"Now wait just a minute," the guard shot back, glaring at Charlie. "Don't you go putting no Indian curse on me, you old bastard! I only did what I had to do, and I ain't going to stand here and . . ."

"Now shut up!" Tate snapped at the guard. "I hear

just one more word out of you I'll be tempted to put a curse on your skull with this pistol butt!"

The guard looked sullen and backed away.

Charlie turned to the sheriff and asked, "What will you do with Seth?"

"I guess we'll bury him down at Copeland. I think his pappy is buried there. So far as I know Seth was alone, and there's nobody who should be informed about this."

It took all of them to lift Seth from the ground, and it was a slow journey from the palm hammock back to the muddied water of Gopher Creek.

Seth was buried the next afternoon in the little cemetery at Copeland, close by the grave of his father. Only five people were there, Billy Joe and Watsie, Charlie and Lillie, and Sheriff Tate. A preacher unknown to Seth said the standard funeral words and then the plain casket was lowered into the ground.

When everyone went back to the cars, leaving the small plot again silent, Charlie took a brown paper bag from the pickup and walked back into the cemetery. He kneeled down and placed beside the fresh grave a piece of fried fish and a can of beer. It was the custom of the Seminole to provide a departing friend with that which he had cherished most.

SIXTEEN

CHARLIE WAS SITTING on the bank of the creek, thinking of the simple wedding ceremony he had witnessed that afternoon in the Baptist Church on the reservation, when the first hard rumble of thunder came out of the north. The wind picked up quickly, and lightening flashes streaked from a high bank of black clouds boiling southward. Charlie got to his feet as a few raindrops pelted down, making little puffs in the dry dust.

In a few minutes the rain came in a downpour. Charlie sat in the chickee and listened as the water pounded onto the thatched roof. It was raining so hard he couldn't see the bank of the creek. The ever present cooking fire sputtered vainly and went out, sending up a spiral of hissing steam. Soon the dead coals were riding the crest of a small riverlet, moving steadily from the chickee and in the direction of the creek.

The heavy rain lasted late into the night, starting a flow of water again. On the marsh north of Gopher Creek, the pesticides and the deadly arsenic trickled slowly into the creek, mixed with the now muddied water, and flowed to the west and the south.

When Charlie went down to the dugout the next morning he noticed dead fish floating on top of the water. He also saw a dead turtle and a small alligator dying on the bank. He poled quickly up the creek and found more dead fish and turtles and alligators. This puzzled him greatly, and he knew that something must be terribly wrong with the water.

When he returned to his landing Billy Joe was there to see if they needed anything from the store in Copeland. He had already been down to the creek and had seen the dead fish. He said to Charlie, "Don't drink any of that water, Pappa. And don't use it for cooking. We'll bring water to you from the well."

"I do not understand this strange thing," Charlie said, looking again at the creek. "I have never seen such as this before."

"When I get to Copeland I'll call Fred Henderson and tell him about this," Billy Joe said. "Maybe he will know what it is and what we must do." His face was also deeply puzzled as he got into the truck and drove away.

Charlie stayed around the chickees all that morning, and just after noon Fred Henderson arrived in a van truck with another man. The van was a portable laboratory operated by the game and fish commission. The men took a sample of the water and several dead fish into the van. After an hour they came outside again.

Henderson said to Charlie, "You haven't got a couple of cups of coffee, have you, Mr. Charlie?"

"We have plenty." He poured three mugs and they took seats at the table.

Henderson took a deep drink, then he said suddenly, "This isn't creek water we're drinking, is it Mr. Charlie?"

"No, it is rain water."

Henderson look relieved.

Charlie then asked anxiously, "Do you know yet what is wrong?"

"We've got a good idea," the biologist said. "I'll have to run a few more tests before we know everything, but we know now there's poison in the water."

"It is not a natural thing, then?" Charlie asked.

"No, it's definitely not natural. There are traces of arsenic in it."

Charlie turned to Henderson. "Could someone have poisioned the creek purposely?" he asked.

"I don't know," Henderson said, deeply concerned, "but we're sure going to try and find out. I've got an idea this is coming from something those land developers are doing. There's just no way arsenic could get into the creek without someone putting it there."

"Don't eat anything from the creek for several days," the biologist said. "The poison may contain itself in the creek proper, but it could spread further into the swamp. You'll have to be very cautious until we complete more tests and tell you it's safe again."

"But we take most of our food from the water," Charlie said.

"You'll have to make do on canned goods," Henderson said. "Maybe it will clear up in a few days."

As soon as the men were gone Charlie poled the dugout down the creek toward the swamp. For several hundred yards below his camp there were more dead fish. When he returned to the landing Lillie was waiting there for him.

"Gumbo is sick," she said with anxiety. "He was eating one of the dead fish from the creek, and something is wrong with him."

"Where is he now?" Charlie asked quickly.

"He is lying beside the storage hut."

Charlie found the 'coon and knelt beside it. He knew immediately that the little animal was dying. Foam was coming from its mouth, and its body was jerking violently. Its feet were pawing the dirt frantically, as it had often done to Charlie's head when it wanted food or attention. He cupped the animal's head in one of his hands and stroked its body. For a moment Gumbo seemed to relax, and then he went into a deep convulsion and died. For several minutes Charlie sat on the ground, holding the animal on his lap. Then he got up and placed the body on the floor of the storage chickee.

Later that afternoon Billy Joe came to the chickees with a barrel of well water. "Did Fred Henderson come?" he asked Charlie.

"Yes, he came with another man. They tested the water and the dead fish."

"Did he say what is wrong?"

"Someone has poisoned the water."

"Poisoned it?" Billy Joe said in disbelief. "Who could do that?"

"They do not know, but will try to find this out. There will be more tests also, but we cannot eat anything from the creek."

"Don't worry about that, Pappa," Billy Joe said. "I'll bring meat. It's too bad we never did get a line run to that refrigerator. You could sure use it now." The refrigerator still sat unused by the sewing platform. Billy Joe had canceled the order for the electric line when he learned they would have to move.

Charlie said, "This is a bad thing, Billy Joe."

"Yes, it is bad, Pappa, but we won't have to put up with this kind of thing much longer. I have been offered a job on the Brown Brothers Ranch and have rented a small house in Immokalee. We will be moving from here in about ten days."

"It is a bad thing," Charlie said absently, as if speaking to no one in particular.

He did not tell Billy Joe about Gumbo, and when he was alone again he sat on the ground and stared at the waters of the creek. Lillie had cooked a vegetable stew and a fresh corn pone, but he ate only a bite. Grief was coming to him too swiftly to bear or understand, and he wanted only to be alone.

That night he took several boards from the storage chickee and sat by the fire, building a small coffin. When he finished he put Gumbo inside, then he took the gourd rattle, broke it in half, and dropped it into the coffin beside the animal. After sealing the coffin he put it into the storage chickee.

Charlie did not eat his bowl of corn grits the next morning or drink a mug of the steaming coffee. He put the little coffin, an axe, and some rope into the dugout and moved away down the creek. There were more dead fish and turtles and alligators; death seemed to have advanced further into the swamp.

He moved steadily, not noticing the birds as they flapped away or the otter catching a water snake for its breakfast. He was now past the range of the poison, but he did not notice this either. The dugout moved quickly through the swamp and into the great marsh.

When he entered the River of Grass he turned east and then south until he came to a large hammock surrounded by a thick growth of mangrove trees, their grotesque roots spreading out and running down into the water like the legs of spiders. Hurricanes of past years had smashed many of the limbs down into the brackish water, and now the rotten-egg smell of decay was overwhelming. He rammed the dugout into the mass of splintered limbs and stepped into the water, carrying with him the coffin, the axe, and the rope. When he had picked his way through the mangroves and stepped onto solid ground, he was no longer Charlie Jumper the old Seminole living beyond his time but was Charlie Jumper the Seminole in the days when there were no modern times.

The hammock was covered with live oaks and cabbage palms, and placed about on the ground at random there were many caskets with cypress frames above them, some still upright and some sagging and some fallen. This was the ancient burial ground of his tribe.

After placing the coffin on the ground he cut a small cypress and built two X-frames, binding them with pieces of rope. Then he put one pole on top to hold them upright. He placed the frame over the coffin and left a brown paper bag of crawfish beside it.

The journey back through the sawgrass was as automatic as it had been to the hammock, and when he reached the line of trees that marked the beginning of the swamp he turned to the right and went to the place where he had taken Timmy to see the royal palm grove and the ancient machete encased in the dead trunk.

He walked to the somber tree and struck it with the axe. Then he struck it again and again, smashing into the dead wood until the trunk toppled backward and crashed to the ground. The machete was now free, and he grasped it in his hand and walked back to the dugout. Suddenly he spun around and around, faster and faster, and when he let the machete go it sailed high into the air, tumbling over and over like a flipped coin. When it reached its peak it hung for a moment, and then it came straight down and splashed into the dark water.

For a few moments he watched silently as the ripples spread outward from the spot where the machete had disappeared; then he suddenly screamed, a wild shrill scream that shattered the quietness of the glade and ricocheted into the swamp. He got into the dugout and moved away quickly.

When he reached the chickees Lillie had cooked a beef roast Billy Joe had brought. Although this was one of his favorites, he ate little. For several hours he sat by the fire, staring into the darkness of the swamp.

SEVENTEEN

Dawn crept into the swamp as usual, quietly and without fanfare, at first a steel-gray and then a mixture of orange-red. The birds flew from their night roosts in search of food as the alligators returned to the mudbanks to rest after a night of hunting. The fish moved now, striking at bugs on top of the calm water and chasing minnows into the clumps of pickerel weeds with their blue flags glistening with dew. The squirrels barked as the 'coons and 'possums clambered down from the trees, and high above it all, the crows screamed loudly as if trying to awaken the swamp itself.

Charlie sat on the bank of the creek and watched this awakening, but his eyes did not reflect anticipation as they always had at this time of day. His face was solemn, and he moved as if very tired.

When it became light in the clearing he went to the storage chickee and took out a rifle wrapped in a tight covering of deer hide. It was a model 1870 Winchester that had been given to him by a friend when he was very young. He had never known if the rifle had been found in the swamp or stolen from some white hunter's camp, and he had used it little except for a few times hunting bear.

After examining a box of shells he loaded the chamber and put the rifle in the dugout. Lillie watched in puzzlement. It had been many years since he last touched the gun, and she knew he would not this day hunt the bear.

He moved through the floating bodies of the fish and past the turtles and small alligators that had crawled onto the bank to die. The herons and the water turkeys flapped out of his path, squawking loudly to protest this intrusion. He crossed the dwarf cypress swamp quickly, moving directly towards the pond where Little George lived. He did not stop along the way to spear any garfish.

When he reached the pond he stopped the dugout just off the mudbank. Then he stood ramrod straight and looked into the one eye of the giant alligator. Neither man nor alligator moved for several minutes; then he picked up the rifle and aimed.

When the bullet struck, the alligator remained motionless for a split second. Then his body shot straight upward, twisting over and over frantically. He slammed back onto the mudbank on his back, then righted himself quickly. Blood spurted from a gaping hole in his head and ran down the bank, spreading out into a crimson pool in the black water. His body twitched violently. Then he bellowed loudly and lay still.

Charlie dropped to his knees in the dugout and started swaying back and forth, chanting a sound that

had no meaning save to himself. His motion increased its tempo as the blood continued to spread and came nearer the canoe.

He was not aware that the airboat had come into the pond and was now just behind him. Fred Henderson had been passing in the creek when he heard the shot, and had cut the engine and poled the boat toward the sound of the rifle. Amazed and perplexed, he watched as the old man continued to sway back and forth in the bottom of the dugout, the huge alligator still pumping blood down the mudbank.

Henderson pushed the airboat against the dugout and Charlie looked up, his eyes blank. Henderson said, "What in the world have you done, Mr. Charlie?"

"I have killed him, I have killed him," was all that Charlie answered.

"Why, Mr. Charlie? Why?"

"I have killed him. I have killed my friend."

Henderson knew he would not get a coherent response to any question. For a moment he said nothing more. The color had drained from his face, and his hands were trembling. He finally said, "Mr. Charlie, if that was a deer I would just turn my back and go away, but I can't do it with an alligator. I just can't, Mr. Charlie. Do you understand what I am saying?"

"Do what you must," Charlie said without any trace of emotion. "I have killed my friend."

"God knows I hate this, Mr. Charlie, but there's nothing else I can do. I'll have to place you under arrest."

"What will you do with the alligator?" Charlie asked, this seeming to be his only concern.

"One that big—they'll probably give the hide to the museum in Naples. I've never seen one like him before. I didn't know there was a 'gator that big still left in the swamp."

"He has lived long, and his body was his life. You will not leave him here then?"

"No, Mr. Charlie. I'll use ropes and pull him out with the airboat. You go on back home and I'll see you there later."

Charlie seemed greatly relieved that Little George would not be left in the swamp to rot and be eaten by vultures. He did not look again at the mudbank. As he pushed the dugout out of the pond, Henderson shook his head in bewilderment.

Three hours later the warden arrived at the chickees to take Charlie to the branch courthouse and jail in Immokalee. Lillie said nothing. She could only watch silently as they left.

Henderson stopped and told Watsie what had happened and where Charlie would be. He asked that Billy Joe come to Immokalee as soon as he returned home from his job.

Night was just beginning to fall when Billy Joe arrived at the one-story building that served as a branch courthouse and jail for the eastern section of the county. The parking area was deserted, and the outside lights had come on around the building. Two green patrol cars were parked near the rear entrance.

Billy Joe had never before been involved with a law enforcement officer or a jail or a courtroom, and his fear now was overwhelming. He did not understand what his father had done, yet he knew that Charlie would never commit such an act without reason.

He walked to a desk in the lobby and asked the officer on duty, "Do you have Charlie Jumper here?"

The man looked up from a magazine he was reading. "Is that the one Henderson brought in for shooting an alligator?" he asked.

"Yes. He is my father. Can I see him?"

"Yeah. He's the first one we've had in here for poaching since the new law was passed. Just come on back with me."

Billy Joe followed the man through a double door and to a cell along a white corridor. Charlie was sitting on a wall bunk. He looked very small and very old, and there was now fear in his eyes. When he saw Billy Joe he got up and came to the cell door.

"Pappa, what is this thing you have done?" Billy Joe asked.

"I killed the alligator," Charlie said simply.

"But why, Pappa? Why did you do this? Did he attack you and force you to shoot him?"

"I was in no danger."

Billy Joe stood silent for a moment, and then he said, "I'll go see Mr. Lykes. He'll help us. I'll be back as soon as I can."

He followed the officer back to the front desk and asked, "What will happen now?"

"Well, if he pleads guilty he can be tried here in the justice of the peace court. He can put up bond now and come back for the trial in the morning."

"What would happen after he pleads guilty?"

"The law's been changed, you know. Killing a 'gator is a felony now, and he could get up to five years in prison plus a stiff fine. He's in some pretty bad trouble."

A lump formed in Billy Joe's throat when he heard this, and for a moment he thought he would gag. "I'll be back as soon as I can," he finally managed to say.

Albert Lykes was just leaving his office when Billy Joe parked in front of the building. He said, "Hello, Billy Joe. What brings you up here this late in the day?"

"Pappa is in jail, Mr. Lykes."

"What's he charged with?" Lykes asked, startled by the stark fear in Billy Joe's eyes.

"Killing an alligator."

"Killing an alligator?" Lykes repeated, puzzled. "Have you talked to your father yet?"

"Just briefly in the jail."

"Did he say why he did this?"

"No, he didn't. He would only say that he killed the alligator." Billy Joe paused for a moment, then he said emphatically, "But Pappa would never do a thing like this without reason, Mr. Lykes. You've got to believe that."

"What reason could there be, Billy Joe?" Lykes asked, becoming even more perplexed by the whole situation.

"I don't know, but something must have made him do it. We'll just have to find out why."

"Who made the arrest?"

"Fred Henderson, the game warden."

"The only thing your father can do here is plead guilty and go before the justice of the peace. That way he's almost certain to get a stiff sentence. I'll post his bond and ask for a jury trial in Naples, then I'll talk to Henderson and find out what this is all about. I believe the court meets next Monday in Naples."

Billy Joe walked to the pickup as Lykes got into his car. He turned the truck and followed Lykes back along the now deserted streets toward the jail.

EIGHTEEN

IT WAS TWO DAYS before Albert Lykes could get away from his office and drive to the swamp to talk to Charlie Jumper. Fred Henderson had told him about the poisoned creek and how they had traced it to the actions of the land clearers. He surmised that in some way the two incidents were connected; but if this one possibility proved to be negative, then he had no idea what he would do.

It seemed to Lykes that with all the punishment the white man had already inflicted on the Seminole they should not bring Charlie Jumper into court even if he had killed a boxcar full of alligators. But Lykes was lawyer enough to realize that he would have to base his defense on something more concrete and more positive than what had happened in the past to the Seminole.

Lykes' spirits were a degree higher that morning than they had been during the past few weeks. He had received a letter from the governor concerning his Big Cypress editorial campaign, and he knew now that his articles and editorials had generated letters that had at least been noticed and read outside the city limits of Immokalee. The governor wrote that he had been concerned for some time about the plight of Big Cypress and the Everglades, but there was not much the state could do about how private property was developed. He would, however, study and pursue the possibility of the federal government and the state jointly purchasing as much as possible of the swamp and either creating a wildlife refuge or making it a part of the National Park. Lykes thought that this was at least a faint glimmer of hope, that finally someone was now looking and listening, but he also knew it might already be too late.

He had taken one action that, if successful, would preserve at least ten acres of swamp so that in future years people could come and look and marvel at what this entire land had once been. Seth had died with no will and no heirs; thus his property would go to the state. Lykes had petitioned the state to make the property into a park after the land development around it was completed. He remembered once when he had been fishing at Seth's camp he had suggested to Seth that he could make money by charging people a dollar each to walk through the stand of virgin bald cypress, just as they pay to see other such spots around the state. Seth had said to him, "A man ought not have to pay to walk in the woods, Mistuh Lykes. God put it there free." He believed that the creation of a nature park from Seth's woods would have pleased Seth, and that the park would be of much more value to everyone than the money the state could get from the sale of the property.

When he reached the chickees Lykes found that although the poison had been stopped the mud-silt had not, and now the once clear little stream was a solid gray, resembling dirty dishwater. He could also see the lifeless bodies of turtles and small alligators rotting on the banks.

Charlie was sitting at the table beneath the cooking chickee, and Lykes walked over to him. He said pleasantly, "Hello, Mr. Jumper. May I join you?"

"You are welcome in my camp," Charlie said, his voice listless. "Would you have coffee?"

Lykes sat down and said, "Yes, thank you."

Charlie poured two mugs and came back to the table. He was not enthusiastic about this visitor, for he knew why he had come and he didn't want to talk about it.

Lykes said, "Looks as if the creek is about shot."

"Yes, the mud has moved another half mile since yesterday. It will soon be in the swamp."

Lykes sensed that he would have a difficult time drawing from Charlie the clue he was seeking. He said, "It's a shame what is happening here, Mr. Jumper. I have fished many times from Seth Thompson's camp, and this was always my favorite place."

"Seth was my friend," Charlie said sadly. "They did not have to kill him."

Lykes felt he was getting further and further away from the old man and that he must change his tack. He said, "Would you show me the place where the alligator lived?"

"If you wish."

Lykes sat in the front of the dugout as Charlie poled them down the creek and finally out of range of the mud. There was no conversation between the two of them as the dugout crossed the dwarf cypress swamp and entered the pond where Little George had lived and died.

They remained silent for a moment more, then Charlie pointed toward the mudbank and said, "It was there."

Lykes could see the impression in the soft mud where the alligator had been. He looked around at the other edges of the pond and the woods surrounding them. The soft filtered light and the stillness of the place reminded him of the interior of a cathedral.

When he looked up again and noticed the pain and the anguish in the old man's eyes, Lykes suddenly realized just what this crime and this trial was all about. He said softly, "If I had been you, Mr. Jumper, I would have done the same thing."

Charlie looked down at him and smiled, the tension and fear and distrust draining from his face.

The trip back to the chickees was then one long and intimate conversation.

NINETEEN

CHARLIE ARRIVED at the courthouse in Naples an hour before the appointed 9 A.M. time to meet Lykes. With him were Billy Joe, Watsie, and Timmy. Lillie had refused to come. Her fear of what might happen was too great for her to leave the sanctuary of the sewing platform. She would spend these anxious hours alone.

The small group stood on the sidewalk in front of the courthouse, waiting in silence. They were soon joined by Frank Willie and Lucy, who had come to be with Charlie during the trial and give what moral support they could.

When Lykes arrived he led them into the building and into the fluorescent-flooded courtroom with its padded seats and polished wood. To all but the small flock brought in by Lykes, this trial was of no importance. The prosecutor had spent only five minutes studying the file, and the judge had merely glanced at the trial on the docket. It would be a routine matter of no significance.

Also in the courtroom were Kenneth Riles, Ron Simmons of Surf Development, and Will Lawton, foreman of the land-clearing crews. Lykes had issued subpoenas to Simmons and Lawton to appear, and both were puzzled since there was no apparent connection between them and a trial for alligator poaching. Riles had accompanied them out of curiosity.

Promptly at ten the judge occupied the bench and Lykes took Charlie to the defense table past a bannister that separated this area from the rows of spectator seats.

To Charlie the preliminaries of beginning the trial were only more things he did not understand, and soon the prosecutor was calling his first and only witness, Fred Henderson, to the stand.

The prosecutor began, "Mr. Henderson, what is your occupation?"

"I am a game warden."

"Did you arrest the defendant, Charlie Jumper, for killing an alligator?"

"Yes, I did."

"Did you actually see him kill the alligator?"

"No, but I arrived moments after the alligator had been shot."

"Could anyone else have committed this act beside the defendant?"

Lykes rose to his feet and said, "Your honor, this line of questioning is unnecessary. We admit that the defendant, Charlie Jumper, did actually kill the alligator."

The judge said, "Well, counselor, if you admit the guilt of your client, what is the purpose of this trial? Why was this case not handled by the justice of the peace in Immokalee?"

"We intend to prove mitigating circumstances, your honor."

The judge asked, "Was your client's life endangered by this alligator?"

"No, sir, it was not," Lykes answered.

"Then I don't understand how there could be mitigating circumstances in a case such as this. I hope you are not wasting this court's time by bringing this case to trial. We have a very busy docket, Mr. Lykes."

"I am aware of that, your honor, and if you will allow this trial to proceed we will establish the defense."

"Very well," the judge said reluctantly. "We will proceed with the trial."

The prosecutor said, "Your honor, if the defense admits the guilt of the defendant, there is nothing more we can ask the witness. We have no more questions."

Lykes got to his feet and said, "As our first witness we call Will Lawton."

Lawton came forward to the stand and was sworn in, then Lykes said to him, "Is your name Will Lawton?"

"That's right, and you know that already," Lawton said belligerently.

"Just answer the questions, Mr. Lawton," the judge cautioned.

Lykes continued, "What is your present occupation?"

"I'm the foreman of several land-clearing crews working for Surf Development Corporation."

"And where are you presently working?"

"At a new project in Big Cypress."

Lykes paused for a moment, then he said, "Mr. Lawton, do you consider yourself to be a responsible man?"

"I don't know what you mean," the foreman responded.

"I mean, do you think things out and take full responsibility for your acts?"

"I always have. I don't depend on nobody else to do my thinking, if that's what you mean."

The prosecutor rose and said, "Your honor, I don't see how the appearance of this witness or this line of questioning has anything to do with the case."

The judge turned to Lykes. "Counselor, what is the purpose of your questions?"

"This witness is pertinent to the case," Lykes said. "If your honor will allow me to proceed I will make the connection."

"Very well," the judge said, "but at this point your questions seem to be completely irrelevant."

Lykes turned back to Lawton and said, "Did you or did you not order your men to place poison in the form of arsenic, as well as heavy pesticides, in a marsh adjoining Gopher Creek?"

"Yeah, I did," Lawton said cautiously, now wondering what Lykes was leading to.

"Why did you do this?"

"My men had complained about snakes in that area."

"Were there also alligators in that area?"

"Yeah, they was some 'gators there too, but the men was mostly concerned with the snakes."

"Do you advocate putting out deadly poison everywhere there is a possibility of snakes?"

"If it takes that to get a job done, yes."

Lykes looked directly at Lawton and said, "Were you not aware that this poison would eventually find its way into the creek and poison the water?"

"What difference does it make if it did poison the creek?" Lawton shot back. "The creek ain't going to be there much longer anyway."

Lykes looked toward the jury box, then he turned to the judge and said, "Your honor, I submit that this man's actions are the direct cause of this trial being held, and that he should be on trial and not the defendant. I also submit that he is guilty of the premeditated murder of not one but more than fifty alligators and countless other species of wildlife. I further submit that he should be charged with criminal negligence and prosecuted with vigor!"

Lawton jumped to his feet and shouted, "I ain't going to sit here and . . ."

"That's enough, Mr. Lawton!" the judge interrupted quickly.

The prosecutor had also jumped to his feet and come to the front of the courtroom. The judge looked at both him and Lykes and said, "This trial is recessed for fifteen minutes while I consult with the prosecutor and the defense counsel in my chambers. You are dismissed, Mr. Lawton."

The prosecutor and Lykes followed the judge to an

office in the rear of the building. As soon as they entered the room the prosecutor said, "What the hell you trying to do, Lykes? You know damned well that Lawton or his actions have nothing to do with this case. Maybe he should be charged and brought into court, but he's not on trial here this morning."

"I think he's got everything to do with the case," Lykes said, "but you won't let me . . ."

"Just a minute, both of you," the judge said. He took a seat in a black leather chair behind his desk. He turned to Lykes and said, "Albert, I read the *Everglades Gazette* every week, and I'm well aware of your personal opinion of the development of Big Cypress. Are you trying to use my court as a soapbox for expressing those opinions?"

Lykes answered, "No, I'm not. There are things that must be brought out if my client is to receive a fair hearing, and that man's testimony was a part of it."

"I still say you are wasting the court's time," the prosecutor said.

"I can assure you I am not," Lykes said firmly. "This man Lawton is vital to the circumstances of my client's actions, but I certainly am not going to reveal to you at this point the whole basis of my defense. If I did that, what's the use of proceeding with the trial? If you will give me time I will bring my case into focus."

"How many witnesses do you intend to call?" the judge asked.

"Only two more. Ron Simmons of Surf Development and the defendant."

The prosecutor said, "I still say that all of this malarkey is a waste of time."

"What the hell is your hurry?" Lykes snapped. "How come you want this trial over so quickly? You want that old man out there sent to jail just so it won't take too much time?"

The judge said, "Let's not get emotional. I've never seen such a ruckus over a simple poaching case."

"This is not a simple poaching case!" Lykes said emphatically. He was surprised himself by the tone he had directed toward the judge.

The judge said, "I'm going to let you proceed, Albert, but you had better bring some relevancy into your case, and do it soon. If you don't, I'm going to overrule you at every turn and put a swift end to this trial. I don't see your point yet, and as I said before, I'm not going to allow you to use my courtroom as a platform to get something personal off your chest. Do you understand that?"

"Yes, I understand," Lykes said.

"Very well. Let's proceed with the trial."

After they returned to the courtroom and the judge was seated, Lykes called Ron Simmons to the stand. Simmons appeared apprehensive and ill at ease. Lykes said to him, "Your name, please?"

"Ron Simmons."

"And your present occupation?"

"I am vice-president of Surf Development Corporation."

"And just what is your responsibility with this company, Mr. Simmons?"

"Public relations and sales promotion."

"Just exactly what do you mean by public relations?"

"Well, you know. Good will. Making the public like us and support our projects."

"Does it make the public like you when you slaughter wildlife?" Lykes asked.

The prosecutor said quickly, "I object to such a question, your honor. It has no point in this trial."

"Objection sustained," the judge said. "You will ask no more questions such as that, counselor."

"Very well, your honor," Lykes said. He turned back to Simmons. "At the present time, Mr. Simmons, do your responsibilities go beyond these public relations duties?"

"Yes. I have been given the responsibility of overseeing the initial land development of Everglades Villas."

"In that case, the men working out there now are your direct responsibility. Is that correct?"

"At this point, yes. But it is only temporary."

"Have you been out to the project to see firsthand what is being done?"

"No."

"Why not?"

"I don't have the time. And besides that, the foreman has that responsibility."

"But isn't the foreman responsible to you?"

"In a way, yes."

"Yet you really don't know what he is doing out there?"

"I know that he is clearing the land, like he is being paid to do. And he is an expert in his job."

Lykes paused a moment, then he said, "Mr. Simmons, did you have any feelings of guilt when the foreman poisoned the creek and all those alligators and other creatures died? Were you concerned about this?"

"I see no point in answering such a question."

"Would you see a point if it had been human beings who died instead of creatures?"

"That would have been an entirely different matter. Of course I would have been concerned."

"Did not one of your guards needlessly shoot to death a human being out there?"

"That's enough!" the judge said harshly. "The witness is excused. This line of questioning cannot proceed." He turned to Lykes. "It is already near noon, and the defense has not yet called a valid witness or established a line of defense. Court is recessed until 2 P.M., and I would like a word with the defense counselor."

Lykes walked slowly toward the bench. He knew he had been legally and ethically wrong on what he had done thus far in the trial, but he also knew he must get certain things into the jurors' minds before he put Charlie Jumper on the stand. And to do this he was willing to risk a lecture from the judge.

When he approached the bench the judge said to him, "Albert, dammit, I gave you leeway and you tricked me! I am not going to stand for any more of these circus antics, and you are not going to use me!

Now you either get on with the direct defense of your client or remove yourself from the case!"

"So help me, John," Lykes said earnestly, "all of this is a valid part of the trial. I have not tricked anyone. You will see the point when I call the defendant to the stand."

"You had better be right!" the judge said sternly.

Lykes left the courtroom with Charlie, Billy Joe, Watsie, Timmy, Frank Willie, and Lucy, and they walked to a small cafe two blocks from the courthouse. They took seats at a table and Lykes said, "Well, what'll it be, everyone? Lunch is on me."

"Could I have the meat that is between the bread and the fried potatoes?" Charlie asked. "I had this once in Immokalee, and it was good."

"That will be fine," Lykes said. He turned to the waitress. "Make it two hamburgers and fries for everyone."

After the order was taken, Billy Joe said, "Mr. Lykes, I don't understand what all that meant this morning. How come the judge and the other man got so angry at you?"

"It was nothing but the way lawyers sometimes play games," Lykes said.

Charlie looked at Lykes and said, "Do not bring trouble to yourself because of me, Mr. Lykes. I have committed the act which they say, and I have told this to Fred Henderson and to others."

"Don't worry about me," Lykes said to Charlie. "I think I can take care of myself in a courtroom. Our concern is with you, not me."

"Are they going to send Granpappa away, Mr. Lykes?" Timmy asked apprehensively.

"I don't know, Timmy," Lykes said slowly. "But don't you worry about your grandfather yet. This trial is not finished by a long way."

When the court was reconvened, Lawton was no longer in the audience, but Riles and Simmons had returned to watch the conclusion of the trial. A group of Billy Joe's and Charlie's friends from the reservation had come late to Naples to witness the proceedings and were now seated in a group in the rear of the room. Fred Henderson had also returned, although his part in the trial was ended.

Lykes rose to his feet and said, "Your honor, we would like to bring a piece of evidence into the court."

"Very well, counselor," the judge said warily, still unhappy with the morning's proceedings.

Two bailiffs brought in the huge alligator hide and placed it on the floor in front of the jury box. The jurors and the judge stared at the enormous size of the hide.

Lykes then placed Charlie on the stand and asked his first question, "Mr. Jumper, how old are you?"

Charlie answered slowly, the fear of being on the stand causing his hands to tremble. "I am not sure, but I know of eighty-six years."

"How long have you lived in Big Cypress Swamp or the Everglades?"

"All of my years."

Lykes pointed to the hide. "Is this the alligator you killed?" he asked.

"Yes, that is the one."

"How can you be sure? There are many alligators and many alligator hides."

"Because of the scar on his head. That is Little George."

"Who is Little George?" Lykes asked.

"The alligator," Charlie said, pointing to the hide. "That is the name of the alligator."

The prosecutor arose and said, "Your honor, this line of questioning is irrelevant to the case and serves no purpose. The name of the alligator is of no concern to the court."

The judge had become mildly interested in this unique presentation tied to the alligator hide, and he wanted to hear more. He said, "You may proceed, counselor."

Lykes then said, "Mr. Jumper, how long have you known of this alligator?"

"Sixty years or more. Little George was very old."

"Would you please tell the court how that scar came to be on the alligator's head."

Charlie spoke slowly, forming his words carefully as if in deep remembrance, "I took the alligator from the swamp when he was but a foot long and kept him in the village. One day a white boy came to the chickees and saw the alligator on the ground. I had never seen this boy before. He took a burning stick from the fire and put it to the back of the alligator's head. The little 'gator screamed like a child, but the boy kept pushing the stick in until he had burned out one eye and set the back of his head on fire. I knocked the stick away, and Little George was almost dead. I made medicine from herbs and roots and mud and kept it on the burned place for many weeks, and the alligator lived. When he became larger I took him to the pond in the swamp and set him free."

Lykes asked, "Did you see the alligator between the time you put him in the pond and the day you shot him?"

"Yes. I would feed him each week. Mostly I would take him the garfish, and sometimes a rabbit. When we had one to spare, I would give him a chicken."

"You mean you have been feeding this alligator each week for sixty years?"

"He was my friend, and he could not see to hunt as well as the others."

Lykes then asked, "Mr. Jumper, what first made you think of killing the alligator?"

"It was because of Gumbo."

"And who is Gumbo?"

"The little 'coon that lived in my chickee."

The prosecutor arose and said, "Your honor, I object again. These questions are irrelevant and a waste of the court's time."

By now the judge was thoroughly absorbed in the proceedings. He said briskly, "Objection overruled. You may proceed with the questioning, counselor."

Lykes focused his attention again on Charlie. He asked, "What did the 'coon called Gumbo have to do with the alligator?"

"When the men who are clearing the swamp poisoned the creek, they killed the fish and the turtles and the alligators. Gumbo ate one of the fish from the creek, and he died. Before he died he was in great pain and suffered much, and I did not want Little George to suffer as Gumbo had suffered."

Lykes then said, "No more questions."

The prosecutor had not intended to cross-examine the defendant, but now decided to do so in order to focus the jury's attention back to the fact that there had been a violation of the law. He crossed to the witness stand and said, "Mr. Jumper, do you believe that this alligator you call your friend would have preferred to live rather than have you put a bullet into its head?"

"He would have liked to live the rest of his life in the swamp, but this was not to be."

"Did you know that the poison would penetrate further into the swamp and kill the alligator?"

"No, I did not know this."

"Then you might have killed him for no purpose. Isn't this right, Mr. Jumper?"

"If he had not been killed by the poison, then he would have been killed by the machines."

"Not all alligators are killed when land is cleared, are they, Mr. Jumper. Many must survive."

"Some would get away, but Little George was very old and could not see as well as the others. He did not know any other place but the pond where he lived, and he would not have left when the machines came. He would have been crushed by the bulldozer, and I did not want him to die in this way or by the poison. He was my friend."

The prosecutor sensed that Charlie's simple, direct answers were having an effect on the jury even beyond his previous testimony. He looked toward the jury box and thought he detected a hostility against his line of questioning. He said quickly, "No more questions."

Lykes arose and said, "We have no more witnesses, your honor. The defense rests."

Charlie came from the witness stand in great relief that his part in this strange drama was ended. He sipped from a glass of water as the courtroom fell silent, waiting for the summations.

The prosecutor knew that he had been put into an almost impossible position, but the fact remained that the law had been violated and he must try to impress this fact into the minds of the jurors. He got up hesitantly, faced the jury box, and spoke without fervor, "Ladies and gentlemen of the jury, the one important fact in this case is that the law has been violated. If we allow a law to be broken and then not convict the guilty party, then we may as well not have the law. A law is either a law or it is not, and that is the only thing for you to decide in this case. There is no possible way for you to rule but guilty." With this brief statement he returned to his table.

Lykes had been trying to plan his summation while the prosecutor was speaking. He concluded that anything he could say would merely detract from the honesty of Charlie's testimony and could actually do harm. He was willing to take his chances with the jury without speaking at all, but he rose and said, "We have admitted that the defendant, Charlie Jumper, did actually kill the alligator in violation of a law. But this violation of the law is not the important thing in this case. The only thing you must consider is whether Charlie Jumper was right or wrong in doing what he did. There are times in life when all of us must act according to what we know is right. I ask only that you consider what he did, and consider what you would have done."

Both the prosecutor and Lykes declined a rebuttal on the summations, and, following the judge's instructions, the jurors filed out to begin their deliberation of the case.

A hushed atmosphere prevailed in the courtroom as one minute passed into five, five into thirty, and a half hour into an hour. To Lykes this was good. He knew that if the jurors were concerning themselves with only the one point of law violation, they would not have been out of the room for more than ten minutes.

Another hour passed, and still the jury box was empty. Long shadows were beginning to form outside the building, and the western sky was streaked with red. Lykes left the table and purchased two sodas from a machine in the hall. Charlie drank the cold liquid gratefully, his face reflecting both apprehension and fatigue. No one left the courtroom. Everyone, even those spectators who were spending the day listening to trials simply out of curiosity and had no personal interest in this case, wanted to remain and hear the verdict.

Lykes was concerned now that the trial might end with a hung jury. If this happened, and a second trial became necessary, he knew he would not have the leeway in a second trial that he had enjoyed in this first. A second trial would be confined strictly to the one point of law violation, and chances for an acquittal would be greatly reduced.

Another fifteen minutes passed; then the jurors filed back into the room. The judge asked for the verdict, and the foreman said, "Your honor, we find the defendant not guilty." Lykes slumped forward against the table, and Charlie looked down at his bare feet.

No one in the courtroom seemed to move or breathe for a moment. Then a sudden outburst of applause came from the spectators and the jury. The judge rapped hard with his gavel. When the noise subsided, he said, "Will the defendant please rise and face the court." Charlie pushed himself to a standing position, and the judge continued, "Mr. Jumper, in a verdict such as this it is not customary for the judge to make further comment. I do, however, wish to issue a word of caution. I would not like to see you back in this courtroom again. You might not be so fortunate the next time. You are now free to go."

For a moment more the courtroom remained motionless, then there was a sudden rush of movement. Billy Joe ran to Lykes and grabbed his hand, and the group on the back row moved in mass to the front.

Charlie was still confused by it all, but he did hear the words "free to go." He moved away from the table as Timmy threw his arms around him. The second to reach him was Lucy, and then Fred Henderson.

Lykes looked around and noticed Kenneth Riles and Ron Simmons standing in the rear of the room. Both looked as if they wanted to come forward and say something to him or to Charlie. They hesitated for a moment more; then they left the building.

Night had fallen when the courtroom was finally cleared. Charlie's entourage of followers went outside to the parking area. They all stood around the dusty pickup, at first discussing the trial with Lykes, then talking about hunting and fishing and the price of cattle and crops and the weather. The bright street lights and flashing neons fascinated Charlie. For several minutes he watched them with interest; then he was swept with an overwhelming desire to leave this place quickly and return to the darkness and the quiet of the swamp.

TWENTY

FOR TWO DAYS AFTER the trial Charlie seemed to be his old self again. He ate his food with relish, and each day he took Timmy into the swamp, exploring the same ponds and sloughs they each had always loved.

On the third morning he came from the chickee wearing the knee-length dress instead of the dungarees. When Lillie looked up from the grill and saw this, she knew. He ate his corn grits and fried beef strips and drank the steaming coffee, then he put his spear and the bow and arrows into the dugout.

He came back to the chickee and said, "It is time to go. Will you come?"

"I am too old," she said, her eyes misty. "I will go and live in the house of Billy Joe."

"You will give the rifle to Timmy."

"I will do this if you wish." She went to the grill and said, "You will need food for the journey."

She wrapped corn bread and beef strips in a piece of brown paper and handed it to him. He took her hands in his and gripped them tightly; then he turned and walked to the dugout.

For several minutes after he was gone she continued to look after him, watching the flow of muddy water and knowing he would not come this way again.

She turned when the pickup came down the dirt path and stopped. Billy Joe came to her and said, "We will be ready soon. Where is Pappa?"

"He is gone."

"Gone where?"

"To seek the island."

After a moment's silence Billy Joe said, "Oh, Mamma, why did you let him go? There is no Forever Island. It is just an old man's memory playing tricks on him. It is only a dream, Mamma."

"You are wrong, son," she said. "It is not a dream. It is pride."

Billy Joe shook his head. "We will go after him. I will get Fred Henderson to help. He cannot survive out there, Mamma."

"He would not survive in the house in Immokalee."

He said again, "We will go after him."

"Let him go, Billy Joe!" she said firmly. "He will return if he wishes."

"But there will be nothing left here for him to return to, and he will not know where we are. Don't you understand that, Mamma?"

"He will find the way."

Billy Joe walked back to the pickup. He turned and said, "Timmy and I will be back for you in about two hours. We will load the things then, and we will talk more about Pappa."

For several moments after he was gone she stood still, listening to the roar of the bulldozer as it came closer. Soon now it would crash over the chickees and smash them into the ground. For a moment more she listened, then she went back to the ancient sewing machine and started making the jacket that would be sold to the souvenir stand on the Tamiami Trail.

If you enjoyed reading this book, here are some other books from Pineapple Press on related topics. To request a catalog or to place an order, visit our website at www.pineapplepress.com. Or write to Pineapple Press, P.O. Box 3889, Sarasota, Florida 34230, or call 1-800-PINEAPL (746-3275).

OTHER BOOKS BY PATRICK SMITH

A Land Remembered. In this best-selling novel, Patrick Smith tells the story of three generations of the MacIveys, a Florida family who battle the hardships of the frontier to rise from a dirt-poor Cracker life to the wealth and standing of real estate tycoons.

Allapattah is the story of a young Seminole in despair in the white man's world. Toby Tiger refuses to bend to the white man's will and fights back the only way he knows how. The word allapattah is Seminole for crocodile, a creature that earns Toby's respect and protection.

Angel City. Made into a TV movie, *Angel City* is the powerful and moving exposé of migrant worker camps in Florida in the 1970s.

The River Is Home. Smith's first novel revolves around a Mississippi family's struggle to cope with changes in their rural environment. Poor in material possessions, Skeeter's kinfolk are rich in their appreciation of their beautiful natural surroundings.

A Land Remembered, Student Edition. This best-selling novel is now available to young readers in two volumes. In this edition, the first chapter becomes the last so that the rest of the book is not a flashback. Some of the language and situations have been altered slightly for younger readers.

A Land Remembered Goes to School by Tillie Newhart and Mary Lee Powell. An elementary school teacher's manual, using *A Land Remembered* to teach language arts, social studies, and science, coordinated with the Sunshine State Standards of the Florida Department of Education.

Middle School Teacher Plans and Resources for A Land Remembered: Student Edition by Margaret Paschal. The vocabulary lists, comprehension questions, and post-reading activities for each chapter in the student edition make this teacher's manual a valuable resource. The activities aid in teaching social studies, science, and language arts coordinated with the Sunshine State Standards.

CRACKER WESTERNS

Alligator Gold by Janet Post. On his way home at the end of the Civil War, Caleb Hawkins is focused on getting back to his Florida cattle ranch. But along the way, Hawk encounters a very pregnant Madelaine Wilkes and learns that his only son has gone missing and that his old nemesis, Snake Barber, has taken over his ranch.

Bridger's Run by Jon Wilson. Tom Bridger has come to Florida in 1885 to find his long-lost uncle and a hidden treasure. It all comes down to a boxing match between Tom and the Key West Slasher.

Riders of the Suwannee by Lee Gramling. Tate Barkley returns to 1870s Florida just in time to come to the aid of a young widow and her children as they fight to save their homestead from outlaws.

Ghosts of the Green Swamp by Lee Gramling. Saddle up your easy chair and kick back for a Cracker Western featuring that rough-and-ready but soft-hearted Florida cowboy, Tate Barkley, introduced in *Riders of the Suwannee*.

Guns of the Palmetto Plains by Rick Tonyan. As the Civil War explodes over Florida, Tree Hooker dodges Union soldiers and Florida outlaws to drive cattle to feed the starving Confederacy.

Thunder on the St. Johns by Lee Gramling. Riverboat gambler Chance Ramsay teams up with the family of young Josh Carpenter and the trapper's daughter Abby Macklin to combat a slew of greedy outlaws seeking to destroy the dreams of honest homesteaders.

Trail from St. Augustine by Lee Gramling. A young trapper, a crusty ex-sailor, and an indentured servant girl fleeing a cruel master join forces to cross the Florida wilderness in search of buried treasure and a new life.

Wiregrass Country by Herb and Muncy Chapman. Set in 1835, this historical novel will transport you to a time when Florida settlers were few and laws were scarce. Meet the Dovers, a family of homesteaders determined to survive against all odds and triumph against the daily struggles that accompany running a cattle ranch.